DIRTY JOB

Dirty Deeds: Book Two
By TA Moore

xo

ROGUE FIREBIRD
PRESS

Dedication

To the Five, all of us for now and always. I love you all and appreciate everything you've done to support and encourage me. And to my mum, who puts up with my brain being away in other worlds a lot!

Acknowledgements

Thank you to Penny Rogers and Brian Holliday for keeping me on the editorial straight and narrow, even in the gross bits! You're getting used to it though. You're going to miss it when I stop writing the ick for a while!

CHAPTER ONE

GRADE HAD A bad feeling about this job.

298 Longwall Ave was just too fucking nice. It was one of the old redbrick mansions, originally owned by mining company bosses, on the outskirts of town. They were technically part of Sweeny, but they didn't want to talk about it. Like when you were a teenager and didn't want to be seen in the same vicinity as your parents.

Not that Grade would know anything about that. He drove his shitty new van—it didn't even have any concealed compartments, but it had been cheap at auction—through the unmanned security gates and slowly up the horseshoe drive. All the windows were lit up, and when he killed the radio he could hear the muted sounds of a party in progress—laughter, the clink of glasses, and the dim strains of some blandly unobtrusive string quartet.

Yeah.

That did not help the sinking feeling that he should have just let Clay's call go to voicemail. He'd thought he was about to get laid, not called out on an emergency job.

Of course, Grade supposed, around here every job was an emergency callout. It wasn't like LA, where he actually had clients who booked slots ahead of time, crime on a schedule. That was another thing you couldn't get in Sweeny, along with good theater and sex that didn't get complicated.

That part was his own fault. Grade knew that. He shouldn't have mixed business and his personal life, but… he'd always been weak for bad ideas. Clay was definitely that. What else he was after a couple of months of casual but frequent sex? That was a rock Grade wasn't about to try and turn over.

Or think about right now. Grade shoved the distraction to the back of his brain as he saw Harry waving him onto the narrow spur road that led around the back of the house. The servants' entrance. Grade grimaced sourly to himself at the familiarity of it. He'd seen plenty of those back in his teens, trailed along behind his mom to help her scrub down toilets and roll rich old shut-ins onto their sides so she could change the bedding under them.

The taste of bleach and menthol flooded Grade's mouth from memory, still undercut with the faint, foul stink of neglect. Money could buy dignity—nurses, medical care, the threat of a lawyer to change a will—but for the ones that couldn't spring for that, his mom's discretion had been the most they could hope for.

Grade pulled in next to the back door, neatly slotted into the space spray-painted onto the gravel. He got out and walked around the back of the van to grab his stuff while he waited for Harry to catch up.

The big man gave him an annoyed look when he finally jogged over.

"You could have given me a lift."

Grade unstrapped his rucksack from the back of the van and threw it over his shoulder. He was used to the weight.

"My mom always told me not to pick up hitchhikers," he said.

Harry unzipped his coat to let the night air in. "Sometimes I see what Clay sees in you," he said.

• 2 •

"His cock?"

Harry flushed. It was a slow, determined burn that started at his collar and headed up. Grade didn't let himself enjoy it. That had *not* been professional. He hadn't socked away all the money he could scrape together over the last two years to get back to LA just to let his standards slip now.

"What's with the audience?" he asked, partially to change the subject, and that was a relevant professional question. "I don't usually consider what I do performance art."

Harry pulled a dour face. "Don't worry about that. I've seen the results," he said. "Nobody needs to see the process. Don't worry. They're all pretty occupied. No one is going to interrupt you. This way."

He jerked his head for Grade to follow him and headed toward the back door. Grade stared at his back for a second as he tried to decide if the uneasy feeling in his gut was worth passing up a couple of grand.

It wasn't. That was the problem with needing money. It made you way too willing to overlook red flags.

Grade sighed, grabbed a pack of PPE from the van, and followed on Harry's heels into a tiled mudroom with two compound bows mounted on the wall and orange hunting vests hung up next to them. No blood on the floor.

"You going to give me a heads-up on what happened?" Grade asked as they headed into a long oak-paneled hall.

Harry shrugged. "You know as much as I do," he said. "You think I get invited to this sort of party? Ezra called and told me they had a situation, then left me outside to wait for you. Down here."

He clomped down two steps and opened a door to a set of steep stairs that went down into a basement. Grade looked at him. Harry rolled his eyes. "If I wanted to kill you," he said, "trust me, I'd do it at a reasonable hour and somewhere convenient."

Grade sighed, but it did sound reasonable. He hitched the bag up more securely on his shoulder and started down the steps. Half of him expected Harry to slam the door behind him just to make him jump, but instead the big man shut it quietly.

There were bloodstains on the stairs. Just a few. Grade made it a point to step around them. The last thing he needed was to take home blood on his sneakers and have to explain to his mom.

"Body at the bottom," Clay drawled from somewhere in the basement.

"I can see that," Grade said.

The dead woman lay on her back where she'd fallen, legs bent at awkward angles on the stairs. One of her red-soled heels had broken on the way down, and the shoe dangled from her toes. The heel of her foot was skinned and bloody from the fall.

A puddle of blood had formed under the back of her head. One of her arms was dislocated at the elbow *and* her forearm broken. The bones pushed visibly against her professionally tanned skin.

Grade stepped over the woman's legs and hopped down the last two steps to avoid the mangled knot of her arm. He caught his balance and looked up. The first thing he saw was Clay, sat backward on a chair as he smoked a cigarette.

Curly brown hair was scraped back from his face, although he'd not gone so far as to shave off his stubble, and he'd swapped his usual baggy T-shirt and jeans for a suit. Most of a suit, at least. He'd shed the jacket at some point, and that left the dusty gray pants and vest over a darker gray dress shirt, with the sleeves rolled back to expose his lean, tattooed arms. He'd pulled the tie out of his open collar and stuffed it into his hip pocket, the dark red strip of silk left to dangle against his leg.

For a second Grade's brain glitched out and his mouth went dry. Well-turned-out wasn't usually his thing, but it worked so hard here that his brain needed the processing power to wire in the new kink.

"What?" Clay asked with a smirk through the thin ribbons of smoke. "You didn't think I owned a suit?"

Grade cleared his throat and tried to ignore the hot pulse of embarrassment behind his temples.

"I know you don't," he said. Then he paused as he heard footsteps overhead and dropped his voice an octave before he went on. "Just wondered who you rolled for that one."

Clay laughed. He didn't seem to care who heard him.

"If the two of you are done flirting?" Ezra growled. Grade nearly jumped at the sound of his voice. He'd been so distracted by Clay he'd forgotten to look and see who else was there. Sloppy. "We ain't got all night."

Grade grimaced at the fact that Ezra had a point. He had a nice dry apology on the tip of his tongue, ready to go, as he turned away from Clay and took in the rest of the basement. The words never made it past his teeth as he caught sight of the man bludgeoned to death on the tiled floor.

Blood and red wine splattered the walls. It had matted in the dead man's gray-brown hair and dried in sticky patches on his battered face. Broken glass glittered dully on the ground next to the body. He wasn't naked, so at least that wasn't where Clay's nice suit had come from.

"What," Grade asked, "the fuck happened here?"

Ezra stepped over the dead man's legs. He had also cleaned up for the night, in black slacks and a matching crew-neck sweater. The heavy buckle on his belt was the only leftover from his usual appearance.

"I need you to make this go away," Ezra said as he jerked his thumb over his shoulder at the bodies, a gold watch peeking from under the sleeve on his right arm as he gestured. "Except they can't just disappear. The bodies need to be found, just not here."

Grade could have guessed that. It probably wasn't fair, but class mattered to corpses too. Hit a certain social strata and problems couldn't be solved by making people just "go away". Some of his colleagues back in LA pegged it at white-collar jobs—accountants and doctors—but Grade would set it at blue-collar. A plumber just vanishes, and even if he had no family, he would have clients chasing him or the bank wanting repayment on a loan.

All those media campaigns where family members and loved ones demanded action from the police? Nothing compared to a financial institution that wanted the all-clear to foreclose on a house.

Habit made his brain click on as he tried to work out what scenario he would need to craft to explain away these two deaths.

Then Clay mildly added, "And they can't be found together."

Grade caught himself, because his "bad feeling" finally had a concrete reason behind it.

"Good luck with that," he said. "But I'm afraid I can't take on any more clients right now."

He hitched his bag up more securely on his shoulder and turned to go. Before he could get far, someone grabbed his rucksack and pulled him back. It turned out to be Ezra.

"The fuck are you talking about?" Ezra growled. "You work for me."

"I freelance for you," Grade corrected him. He yanked his bag out of Ezra's grip. "That means I can turn down a contract, and that's what I'm doing. I'm not getting involved in this. Find someone else to clean this up."

Ezra looked annoyed. "What the fuck is your problem?" he asked. "You didn't even blink when we got you to scrape Buchanan—or whoever he was—off the restroom walls."

"That was business," Grade said. He waved his hand around at the basement. "This? This was personal. I have two rules. Cash up front, and I don't work for amateurs."

Ezra reached into his pocket and pulled out a stuffed white envelope. He slapped it against Grade's chest, hard enough to make Grade stumble. Behind Ezra, Clay narrowed his eyes and got up off the chair, casually swinging it around, out of the way. It would have been romantic, in a way, Grade supposed. Except he wasn't sure whose side Clay would pitch in on here.

"Cash up front," Ezra said and tapped his finger pointedly against the paper. "And you're working for me. If that is a problem for you, then you aren't going to get much work around here."

The crinkle of notes inside the envelope as Ezra pressed on it distracted Grade for a second. A job like this *would* pay well—Grade didn't offer a two-for-the-price-of-one discount—and he needed the money. The new van might be shit, but it had still taken a bite out of his savings. He could...

No. This once, Grade was going to listen to his instincts, not his wallet. He shoved down the temptation to at least look at the money and stepped back.

"Look, you might be the one with cash in your hand," he said to Ezra, "but this isn't your crime scene, is it? This smells like amateur hour, and you can't trust amateurs. They get paranoid, or they feel guilty or do something that makes the cop in charge of the investigation look twice. That's when they get arrested and start throwing my name around to the Good Cop in the interrogation room. I don't plan to spend another year in Sweeny, never mind ten in the Castle. Find another cleaner."

He knew they couldn't. It wasn't like Cargill County could provide enough work for two of them. It barely did for one; otherwise Grade would have had his bags packed and his ticket back to LA in hand.

That wasn't his problem, though.

Ezra grimaced, his lips pulled thin over his teeth, and scowled at Grade. "I don't know what makes you think you have a choice. You think Harry is going to let you leave without my OK?"

They stared at each other for a moment. Before Grade could make a decision on how to answer that question, Clay interrupted the standoff. He put a hand on Ezra's shoulder.

"Ezra, back down," he said, his voice slow and accent thicker than usual. "Grade's like a rat. You don't want to make him feel cornered. Let me deal with it."

Something bleak flickered over Ezra's expression for a moment. He looked like he wasn't entirely sure who Clay would pick if he pushed this either. Mostly sure. They'd been friends a long time, there was *history* there, but for what might be the first time, he wasn't 100 percent. That was a dangerous thought to have in a man like Ezra's head long-term, but right now it was useful.

He shrugged Clay's hand off and stepped back.

"Fuck. You know what? Fine. If you want to sweet talk the little shit into doing his job, go right ahead," Ezra grouched. He pushed the sleeves of his sweater up his forearms, revealing a cheap snake tattoo faded down to blue under the scruff of arm hair, and tossed the money onto the chair Clay had just gotten out of. "I'll go and lie to our... associate... that it's all under control, will I?"

Clay scratched his jaw and shrugged. "It'd probably go over better than the truth."

"Fuck you," Ezra told him. He stalked over to the stairs, shoved the dead woman's arm out of the way with the toe of his boot, and started up toward the door. Halfway there, he stopped and looked down at Grade, who turned to watch him go. "Just remember, cleaner, rats get killed. You should know that better than anyone."

He took the last few steps two at a time and stiff-armed the door open. For a second, he was outlined against the bright hall light, broad shoulders and lean hips all in black, and then he slammed the door shut behind him again.

"It bothers you that he could have gotten blood on his boot, don't it?" Clay asked, his breath warm and smoky in Grade's ear. He slid a hand up under Grade's T-shirt, fingers rough against bare skin. "DNA."

"In principle," Grade said. His voice was dry in his throat, sticky, and he had to clear it. Mind on the job, he reminded himself irritably. Or rather the fact that this wasn't his job. "Not particularly worried if it causes Ezra problems right now."

Clay snorted and stepped back. "If it causes problems for Ezra," he said, "it fucks me up too. This sort of shit has a splash zone. Do you care about that?"

It was that sort of question that made it a bad idea to screw around where you worked. Grade tugged his T-shirt down and turned to look at Clay for a second as he took a draw on his cigarette. It burned down to the filter.

"Not enough," Grade said after a moment's thought.

Clay grinned crookedly as he exhaled smoke. "You really think honesty is the best policy right now?"

Grade shrugged. "You're not going to kill me. That would leave you with three bodies to take care of," he said. "I don't work for amateurs. And there's a party upstairs that's in for a rude surprise if anyone needs an extra bottle of wine. I don't think there's time for anything but honesty."

They both glanced up for a second at the reminder. After a moment, Clay pulled a sour face and flicked the butt of his cigarette onto the floor.

"OK," he said. "This wasn't exactly a professional hit, but you aren't working for the psycho that went to town with a bottle of Cabernet. You work for me and Ezra, and it's off the books. There's no reason for our good friend upstairs to even know your name. It's not like she's going to send you a thank-you card. Once her mess is cleaned up, she's not going to want to think about tonight again."

It *still* felt like a bad idea, but... Grade glanced at the packet of cash on the chair and bit his lower lip. Clay did have a point. If the amateur didn't have any contact with him, they couldn't drop him in it when they inevitably spiraled. The scene was messy, but that's what Grade's clients paid him for. If all they needed was a rub around with an antibacterial wipe... well, after the pandemic, everyone had them in the kitchen.

"You'll make sure your associate doesn't know I exist?" Grade checked.

"Cross my heart," Clay drawled as he signed an X over his chest with his index finger. "And when you're done... I'll make good on that thing you thought I was calling about tonight."

Grade let his bag slide off his shoulder. It hit the ground with a thud.

"I'll hold you to that," he said. "Right now, I assume you're supposed to be at the party?"

"I don't think I'll be missed," Clay said. "This is more Ezra's gig."

"That's your problem. I need you up there," Grade said. He started to unpack the PPE. It rustled as he shook it out absently while trying to think through all the parameters. This wasn't the first death he'd had to re-stage. It wasn't even the first time he'd had to clean up a scene with potential witnesses in residence. It was just a challenge to do both at once with no lead-in to do research or plan. "I'm not exactly dressed to rub shoulders with the sort of people who get invited to parties here—"

"Is this because I didn't ask you to be my date?" Clay asked, wry amusement spread on his voice like butter. "Trust me, you didn't miss anything."

Grade rolled his eyes at the jab and pressed on. "So I need you to get their stuff. Car keys, coats, bags. Anything they'd grab if they had to leave the party suddenly."

"You realize I don't know them, right?" Clay said.

"Ask whoever killed them," Grade suggested. "Presumably, if your friend knew these two well enough to want them dead, they knew if they drive a Tesla or not."

Clay reached down and picked up the envelope Ezra had left behind. He tossed it to Grade, who caught it out of the air. The heft of it in his hand was very satisfying.

"Isn't this what we pay you for?" he said.

Grade checked in the envelope and then folded it over to stick into his back pocket. "Not enough."

Clay snorted and pulled his tie out of his pocket. He looped it loosely around his neck, red tangled through lean fingers, as he headed for the stairs.

"I'll see what I can do," he said. "But I start talking to these people about their cars, they're going to think I'm casing the joint."

"And again, that's your problem," Grade said. "And I meant it, by the way."

Clay turned and dropped into a crouch on the steps so he could see Grade. "Meant what?" He tilted his head to the side and slowly rubbed his thumb over his lower lip. "That you're going to hold me to that promise to fuck you? Don't worry. I'm a man of my word… when I wanna be."

Despite his best efforts to keep his mind on the job, Grade's mouth went dry and his balls tightened under his jeans. He could feel the heat spread up through the nape of his neck as he cleared his throat.

"That too," he said. "But you haven't paid me enough for this job. Getting rid of a body is actually the budget option. If you want a package deal like this—"

Clay held up a hand to interrupt him. "I owe you cock," he said. "You want money, that's Ezra's department."

He pushed himself upright and headed the rest of the way up the stairs. Grade walked over to stand next to the dead woman, feet just off the puddle of blood.

"Yeah, well, tell him to get his department in order. I might have eased up the not-working-for-amateurs rule, but I still get paid up front."

Clay let himself out with a parting shot for Grade as he closed the door behind him.

"Now that sounds like your problem," he said. Then the door clicked shut.

Grade glared up the steps for a moment, then sighed as he looked down at the corpse next to him. Her eyes were open, and he could see the faint wrinkle of a contact lens that had drifted into the corner under one eyelid.

"He paid me enough to move the two of you," he said. "Let's get started on that. If he tries to haggle over the invoice, I can always bring you back."

DIRTY JOB

CHAPTER TWO

CLAY THUMBED A pill into his mouth and washed it down with a mouthful of whiskey. He was about to chase it with a second swallow when Ezra grabbed his forearm. Whiskey slopped over the edge of the tumbler and dripped through Clay's fingers.

"The hell are you doing?" Ezra asked through gritted teeth and a fake smile. "The last thing we need right now is you getting fucked up on something and screwing up."

Clay twisted his arm out of Ezra's grip. He set the glass down on a nearby table—and some petty asshole part of him hoped it was expensive enough to be ruined by a ring on the veneer—and sucked the liquor off his fingers.

"Relax," he said. "It was Tylenol."

"Right," Ezra said. He raised his eyebrows. "Because you'd never do something that stupid?"

Clay rolled his eyes and fished in his pocket for the branded blister pack to flash at Ezra. The scars on his chest didn't hurt—he could feel pressure on them but not much else—but sometimes the ones under the skin cramped and spasmed around his ribs. It felt like wires being pulled about under his skin, like it was being pulled away from the meat so he could be basted.

"I'm not a complete fucking idiot, Ezra. I'm not going to do a handful of uppers in front of the mayor and our district representative," he said as he tucked the blister pack into a pocket of Ezra's slacks. "I did a bump of coke before I left the house."

Ezra pushed Clay's hand away. "Some people would think that was a joke."

That wasn't unwarranted. It wouldn't have been the first time Clay had done something along those lines. It meant the high had time to mellow out, taking the edge off but not the clean thread of focus that kept his brain like clockwork.

It also put a short fuse on his temper, but that wasn't always a problem.

"Calm down," Clay said. "I came on the bike."

He'd had the Harley longer than he'd known Ezra. From before a recruiter convinced him boot camp was a better bet than trying to talk his way out of the debt he owed a local dealer. It had been the only thing he'd left in Louisiana that he'd bothered to go back and get.

It got treated better than Clay treated himself. He definitely didn't drive it under the influence. Ezra knew that, and he gave a brief nod of acknowledgement as he turned his attention back to the party that idled around them. Men and women in sedate cocktail outfits sipped champagne and traded gossip in arch voices as they waited for the big event.

"Yeah, well, how was I supposed to know that?" Ezra grouched. Then he changed the subject abruptly. He wasn't good at apologies. "What about your boyfriend? Did he agree to do his job or not?"

"Grade's not my boyfriend," Clay said. He picked his tumbler back up, the crystal heavy and slick in his hand, and took a drink. "Just someone I fuck occasionally."

Ezra reached out and plucked a flute of champagne from a passing waiter's tray. He took a sip as he asked, "So? What's the difference?"

"I don't know," Clay said. He'd never really thought about it before. "A conversation?"

"I'll bear that in mind."

The string quartet tucked into the corner of the room let the music fade down into silence and sat back in their chairs. A man in a well-tailored suit stepped into the middle of the room and clinked a spoon against his champagne glass for attention.

"Should I be jealous?" Clay asked quietly. The rest of the room and out into the hall went quiet as the other guests turned obediently toward the sound.

Ezra snorted and tilted his head back as he drained the champagne. "Yeah," he said, a sarcastic lilt to his voice. "Ever since Janet divorced me, I've really missed having someone's hand in my wallet."

Now that he was the center of attention, the man in the nice suit fumbled briefly with his spoon before he tucked it awkwardly into his pocket.

"Thank you all for coming tonight," he said, his voice pitched to carry, "but I know that none of you came to see me. So let's raise a glass to the woman of the hour…"

Clay tuned him out. "I've bad news for you about that," he said in an aside to Ezra.

"Keep it to yourself."

The man lifted his wine in a toast as he announced, "Judge Charity Parker."

Judge Parker strode through the crowd, hands up to acknowledge the polite applause and a few cheers provided by her guests. She was a fat woman in her fifties, but she didn't play into any of the stereotypes people would assign her demographic. There was nothing soft, cuddly, or fun about Charity Parker. She was all gloss and hardness, from her bob of expensively maintained highlighted blond hair to the gray leather stilettos that took her up to six feet tall.

There was a three-step flight of stairs up to the patio doors that led out to the garden. Charity stopped on the second step and turned to face the crowd.

"Well, unaccustomed as I am to public speaking…" Charity paused long enough to get her laugh. She lifted her hand just as the chuckles started to ebb so she could claim credit for the silence. "Seriously, though, and thank you to my nephew for such a lovely introduction, we all know why we're here, so I won't beat around the bush. After two years in the circuit court, some soul-searching, a lot of hard conversations with my family, and a little Dutch courage…"

She raised her glass in a toast to the room. Clay drained the last of his whiskey and waited for it. The murmur of amused appreciation from the guests died down, and Charity smiled at them.

"I've come to the decision that not only do I have the passion and drive for it, but I have a unique opportunity to represent and advocate for the people of this county," she said. "That's why I intend to run for the Kentucky Supreme Court and will be announcing my candidacy next week."

Clay ran his gaze over the crowd to see if he could pick out the plants with their cued-up applause. He'd been trained for this. Well, to pick out the body in the back of the crowd just about to turn into a mob. The one who was either too clean or too dirty, who didn't have any friends to try and shush him, and who would fade back into the alleys the minute the bottles started to fly.

If only it had been this easy when he was in Afghanistan.

The woman in the blue dress who'd tucked her clutch under her elbow to free up both hands to clap a second before it was due. Toward the back of the room, an older man in an expensively understated suit slid his phone into his pocket just in time to respond to the announcement. A handful of younger guests—mid-twenties to early thirties, either dressed like TikTok influencers or their grandparents—tried to rouse a cheer to go with the applause in perfect unison.

"You've got my vote!"

"Charity begins in Kentucky!"

It wasn't subtle, but it worked. The effusive response from a few spots in the crowd prodded the more sedate guests into following suit. The cheers died down pretty quick, but there was a good ripple of applause and a generally positive murmur of support afterward.

They probably wouldn't be so supportive if they knew about the dead bodies under their feet. People expected public figures to have skeletons in their closet, but corpses in the wine cellar was a different thing altogether.

Nobody liked a wet scandal…

That was a lie. Everyone loved a wet scandal. That was the problem. Charity could probably make any charges go away if she pulled a few strings, but she couldn't stop Jessie Lowry in the laundromat from running her mouth.

With that hanging over her, suddenly Charity Parker wouldn't be such a valuable asset to the people willing to bootstrap her into power.

Announcement made, Charity stepped down and smiled graciously as people clustered around to offer congratulations and wish her luck. Hands were clasped and cheeks were kissed as she made the rounds.

Clay nudged Ezra. "We need to speak with the party girl," he said. "In private."

"Why?" Ezra asked.

"Go over the guest list," Clay said. "Grade needs us to sweep the house, clear up anything our cargo downstairs might have left lying about. If I'm going to do that, I need to know whose shit I'm stealing."

"Don't we pay him to deal with that stuff?" Ezra groused.

"Not enough apparently, but yeah," Clay said. "But I've already had to throw my cock in as a sweetener to get him to agree to the job. So unless you're willing to put a better offer on the table, don't rock the boat."

Ezra gave him a sour look. "You want me to fuck him?"

The quick, jealous catch in the back of Clay's throat at that idea caught him by surprise. He didn't know what that was about. OK, he did. But he'd not zoned out of every appointment he had with the VA's headshrinker to suddenly decide to be emotionally healthy tonight.

Feelings.

They could fuck right off.

Clay smirked at Ezra. "I said 'a better offer.'"

Ezra grunted and started forward through the crowd. "You're lucky I don't fuck where I live," he growled over his shoulder. "And that your boyfriend is the human embodiment of poison ivy. Otherwise, I'd show him what an actual good time is like."

One of the young staffers who'd tried to start the chant caught the tail end of that. He stumbled over his own feet, went red, and gave Ezra a look so frankly horny that Clay almost felt sorry for the kid. He wasn't Ezra's type, not if he worked for

Charity. Ezra liked his men like he liked his ex-wives, full of judgment and too good for him.

"Yeah, you have two kids," Clay said as he stuck to Ezra's elbow. "Your idea of a good time is Disney World."

"It's the fucking happiest place on earth," Ezra said. "And shut up."

He nudged someone out of the way and stepped forward to offer Charity his hand. She hesitated for a moment—her mouth tight under the expertly applied slick of lipstick as resentment flickered murkily through her eyes—and then smiled professionally as she accepted the shake.

"Congratulations," Ezra said.

"A bit premature," Charity demurred on autopilot. "I've not won yet. A lot can happen between here and the polls."

Ezra hung on to her hand a second too long. "Probably won't, though," he said. "By the way, if you can find a couple of minutes? I've an update on that business we talked about."

Charity looked like she'd just swallowed pig swill. It lasted for a second, and then she plastered her social mask back over it. Her lips crimped into a fake indulgent smile, and the powder creased around her eyes as she squinted them.

"Of course." She took her hand back. "I've always got time for one of our proud veterans, Mr. Adams. Just make an appointment with my office next week."

She turned her shoulder to him to accept a "small token of appreciation" from a starstruck college student over some sort of scholarship. The two of them traded pleasantries across the small, neatly wrapped box, and Clay turned away just before someone's flash went off.

That was another thing his time enlisted had taught him, although it had been more trial and error than training. If it was "good" for a guaranteed viral social media post—dead civilians, friendly fire, fuckups—it was not good for the military. So if you couldn't keep the cameras out, at least keep your own fucking face out of frame.

Next to him, Ezra had done the same thing as he grabbed a frothy bit of something on a cracker from a passing tray. They waited out the quick flurry of snaps—Clay figured he could catch it on Twitter later—and then turned back.

Clay stepped between Charity and a well-dressed middle-aged man with a cross tie pin on his silk tie.

"Sorry," he said with a warm smile to the man, who glared at him. "I have to steal the judge away for a second. We just need her to sign some paperwork for the mission so we can stop those good Christian babies from being born in China."

The man blinked and looked confused.

"What?"

Clay slapped the man on the shoulder, hard enough to stagger him. "See? I knew you'd understand." He turned and ostentatiously offered the crook of his elbow to Charity. "Your Honor?"

She glared at him for a second, then visibly softened her face as she turned to the cock-blocked religious lobbyist. A quick, warmly couched excuse soothed his ruffled feathers and sent him on his way. Once he was gone, Charity smoothed her dress down, a slow, controlled gesture with both hands, and checked quickly that no one was near enough to eavesdrop.

"Meet me in the study," she said and then plastered the charm back on as she clasped hands and made excuses on her way out of the room.

"Good Christian babies?" Ezra said.

"It worked, didn't it?" Clay countered as he offered Ezra the arm Charity had ignored. "Shall we?"

Ezra shook his head and slapped the offered arm away.

"Just try and remember that not everyone finds the asshole schtick cute," he said as he started after the judge.

Clay scratched his jaw with his thumb, the stubble rough under his nail, as he watched Ezra walk away.

"Who thinks it's cute?" he asked dubiously. Then he shrugged the question off and followed on Ezra's heels.

§

"Melanie Ledger," Charity said. She poured herself a glass of wine with a steady hand. "And Franklin Collymore. She came alone. He was with his wife, but she left before him. Their nanny had some sort of family emergency? She took an Uber, so he'd have taken the Lexus when he left."

She hadn't asked them to sit down. Clay did anyhow, slouched in the leather armchair next to the heavy antique filing cabinet Charity had sourced her wine from a second ago. His boots scuffed up the pile on the heavy cream rug that covered most of the floor.

"What about Melanie?" he asked. "What did she drive?"

Charity lifted the glass to her mouth and took a long, thirsty drink. Then she wiped the excess off her lower lip with her thumb, the approachable soft apricot color smeared over the pad. She swallowed hard and set the glass down on the desk.

"A gray Bentley," she said. "Her bag will be in it. The keys too."

"My kind of woman," Clay said. "Expensive tastes and easy to rob."

Charity gave him an unimpressed look. She rubbed her finger against her forehead, just above the arched line of her perfectly manicured eyebrow. "Don't get me wrong, but I asked you to do a job, to solve a problem for me, not to audition for the role of my catty gal pal. I don't want to associate with you people any more than I have to. So can we get on with this?"

You people. That never meant anything good.

Clay twisted around to look over at Ezra, who had stationed himself in front of the study door with his arms crossed.

"Does she mean us?" he asked.

"You, maybe," Ezra said mildly. Too mildly if you knew Ezra as well as Clay did. "I'm a pillar of the goddamn community, Clay. Ask anyone."

Charity made a disgusted sound. "Don't pretend you're offended," she said. "We all know what you are."

"Same as you," Clay said. "Or does our money suddenly get clean once it passes through your hands?"

Charity gave him a thin slice of a smile. "That's what I have accountants for." She snatched her wineglass up and slopped wine over her fingers. The red liquid dripped onto the desk as she cursed under her breath and switched hands. "I gave up being idealistic about the law the first time I ran for office and saw how the meat grinder worked. We do business, you and me. That doesn't mean I have to enjoy your company, any more than you do mine. Now can we get on with this? If my career tanks because I snubbed half my supporters, I might as well have just called my lawyer instead of asking you to deal with it, Ezra. Her hourly rates might be extortionate, but we're done once I pay her invoice."

She drained what was in her glass in one gulp. Then she shook the wine off her fingers with an irritated flick of her hand.

Clay looked around at Ezra and raised his eyebrows expectantly. It took a second, but then Ezra shrugged and gave him the nod to get on with it.

Clay pushed himself out of the chair in one quick, smooth motion. Despite her poise, Charity stumbled back a step in alarm. He grinned at her, wide and lazy.

"Coat check?"

She stared at him for a second, but then she waved her hand out the window. "They set up in the garage," she said. Her composure slipped for the first time, and she licked her lips. "What... what... exactly are you going to, um, do with the bodies?"

The memory of Buchanan—well, who they'd *thought* was Buchanan at the time—chopped up so he'd fit in the barrel flickered through Clay's mind. He grimaced at the unsettled feeling it left in his gut.

He'd done worse. Grade might turn corpses into Spam, but Clay made the corpses to start with. It still left him a bit disturbed to think about it.

"Yeah," Clay said. "You don't want to know."

He turned to go. Ezra pushed himself off the door and stepped out of the way. They were about to go out into the hall when Charity broke the silence.

"Aren't you going to ask what happened?" she asked.

Clay traded a wry look with Ezra—it was always the way; people practiced their lies for so long that they felt hard done by if they didn't get to tell them. He turned back.

"No," he said. "Not like I was going to vote for you anyhow."

He closed the study door on her frown.

DIRTY JOB

CHAPTER THREE

GRADE WENT THROUGH the dead man's pockets.

He emptied out an iPhone with a broken screen, a single AirPod—the tiny sound of a streamed podcast still just about audible—and a wallet with a couple of credit cards and a bloodstained scrap of folded-up paper. He smoothed it out, glanced at the writing, and handed the claim ticket to Clay.

"If anyone asks, say he asked you to grab it for him," Grade said. "You're an invited guest, so no reason that should cause any suspicion."

Clay laughed. "Are you kidding?" he asked as he tucked the scrap of paper into his pocket. "Have you met me? I'm enough reason for suspicion."

Grade slid the phone and wallet back into the man's jacket. The fabric was sticky as the blood started to cool. He stood up and snapped his gloves off.

"Just try not to be memorable." He rolled Clay's sleeves down and buttoned the cuffs. "Eye witness testimonies are notoriously unreliable. By the time anyone questions the coat check clerk, all he'll remember is some guy in a suit."

Clay leaned forward and grazed a kiss over Grade's mouth. It was just a tease of warm lips and liquored breath.

"Hot guy in a suit," he said. "Admit it. You want me."

It wasn't the time or the place, Grade tried to remind himself of that, but he still leaned into Clay as he tried to catch the kiss on offer. He caught himself and stepped back, his throat dry as he cleared it.

"It's not like there's a lot of competition," Grade said. "It's you or a guy I once saw chug a quart of used vegetable oil on a bet. So…"

Clay just smirked. He dropped his hand to the waistband of his trousers and flicked his thumb over the button.

"You want to fuck me in the suit," he said confidently. "Just admit it."

Grade narrowed his eyes in annoyance. There wasn't time for this. He had to move two *intact* corpses, clean the scene, and script a new death for both on the drive back into town. That would account for his time right into tomorrow. He couldn't waste time denying the obvious.

"Maybe," he said.

Clay snorted as he unbuttoned his cuffs. "Definitely." He folded his sleeves back up his forearms deliberately.

"The ink, they'll remember," Grade said.

Clay just shrugged. "That's OK," he said. He pulled the ticket out of his pocket and held it up, pinched between two fingers. "I'm going to make Harry do that anyhow. Car theft is more my wheelhouse."

That got Grade's mind out of the gutter. More or less. He waved an exasperated hand at the splattered cellar.

"I need an extra pair of hands," he said. "Unless you know someone else at this party willing to haul corpses around, that means I need Harry."

"It's a coat," Clay said. "How long can it take him to steal it?"

§

Twenty minutes.

The dead woman's heels bounced down the stairs as Grade got her under the arms and pulled her across the room. The tail ends of her hair trailed through the puddle of blood that had leaked out of the back of her head.

Twenty minutes, and—Grade let the body drop once they were clear of the stairs and checked his watch—counting. He wasn't going to hold his breath. He had a feeling that Harry wasn't exactly motivated to hurry back. So far he'd already managed to miss dealing with the mess of the man's corpse, currently wrapped up like a plastic burrito and propped up in a seated position in the corner of the room. Drag it out another ten minutes and all he'd have to do was help carry them out to the van.

The second plastic sheet was already laid out on the floor, taped down at the corners to keep it neat. Grade put his foot against the body's hip and shoved to roll her onto the sheet. She flopped onto it, arms and head slack, and ended up flat on her stomach, her face mashed against the floor. Grade manhandled her onto her back to avoid as much disruption to the already settled lividity as possible. It would still be obvious to a competent pathologist that she'd been moved, but the truth was most bodies didn't get the *CSI: Vegas* treatment.

Not even in Vegas, never mind in Sweeny.

Half-trained cops. Budget constraints. A shortage of fully qualified forensic pathologists who could actually do the job. There were a lot of obstacles between a dead body and the pathologist's knife.

Grade's plan was never to fool the science; he didn't have the background or, usually, the time for that. No, he aimed at giving an overworked and underpaid deputy the opportunity to let something slip through the cracks. If that failed, the second line of defense was just to make it a mess for whoever caught the case.

In LA County, 46 percent of homicide cases went unsolved. Grade would rather get a "no suspicious circumstances" on the file, but he'd settle for a cold-case stamp if he had to. Most of the time, he got it.

Of course—Grade stepped away from the body to get a sterile swab out of his kit—the fact his clients knew how the system worked had helped his stats there. He just hoped this case wasn't going to tank them.

Grade shook that thought out of his head. The time to second-guess himself had been roughly thirty—he checked his watch again—eight minutes ago, before he'd started work. He'd waived his rules and taken the contract. No one had forced him. Now he just had to do the best job he could and make sure that whatever happened, there was nothing to tie him personally to this case.

There were a few different crimes that Grade could be charged with. Desecration of a corpse. Accessory after the fact. Tampering with evidence. The state would probably go with the catchall "obstruction of justice," and Grade would be looking at at least five years in prison.

In Kentucky.

The plastic crinkled under his knees as he knelt on it and tilted the woman's head back. He thoroughly cleaned out both her nostrils with either end of the swab. The cotton tip came out stained brown from old blood and decorated with particles of dust and bits of fluff.

It made Grade's nose itch. He resisted the urge to rub it as he dropped the swab into his makeshift trash can. The nails next. He picked up her hands and turned them over, her skin very white against the blue of his gloves. She had a glossy navy gel manicure, and two of her nails on her right hand were snapped off down to the tender, raw, quick.

Grade set a folded sheet of blank paper on the woman's chest and laid her hands on it. He got his pocketknife and flicked the blade open. It got a quick swipe with an antibacterial wipe, just in case, and then he cleaned under the unbroken nails with a series of quick, businesslike strokes. Gray dust, bits of dry skin, and a few flecks of paint were picked out and dropped onto the paper. He finished, folded the paper in on itself, and tossed it into the can with the swab.

He set the woman's hands neatly on her stomach and repeated the same process with her feet. She'd lost the nail entirely from the little toe on one foot. Grade also gave her bloody heel a quick scrub to remove anything that might have gotten lodged in the skin during her fall. It paid off. He felt something catch on his glove as he worked. Not enough to rip the latex, but definitely not just hard skin.

"Let's see," he muttered to himself as he pushed her leg up. Rigor mortis hadn't set in. He probably had another couple of hours before he had to worry about that, give or take when they'd been killed. The overhead lights—spotlights sunk into the ceiling—were good enough that he didn't need to get his flashlight. He probed at the bloody flesh with his thumb until he felt something under the skin. A splinter, maybe.

It was strange. Grade could take a body apart like it was a roast chicken and feel nothing. The corpse didn't, after all. But he had to bite his tongue on the urge to apologize as he squeezed cooled, torn skin between his thumbs until he saw the dull head of something poke out of the raw flesh.

He knew why… *Dory at the kitchen table, her hands palms up on her knees as Grade blotted away blood and tweezered out chunks of wood. He muttered "sorry" with every new sliver he found dug in under her nails and the heels of her hands. Dory never flinched, though…* but that didn't help much.

Grade caught the tip of his tongue between his teeth and used the point of his knife to work the foreign object out. He caught it as it dropped and turned it between his fingers. Not wood, after all. A brad nail that must have come loose on the stairs. That could have raised questions. Grade wiped it clean and dropped it in with the rest of the things he needed to burn.

He leaned up to peel the woman's lips apart with his fingers. One tooth was gone. From the nub that stuck out of her gum, it had been a crown. Grade grimaced and pried her mouth open to check. He swept his finger around the inside of her mouth, under her tongue, and into the pockets of her cheeks.

No tooth.

Shit.

He pulled his hand back and wiped it on his leg. The red smears left on the fabric weren't from her lipstick.

Grade leaned his elbow on his knee and stared at the dead woman's face as he weighed up the next step. The odds were she'd swallowed it, but there was no way to know for sure. He bounced his heel absently as he tried to put himself in the mind of a deputy sheriff. Would a broken, missing crown raise enough suspicion to make it worthwhile pushing for an autopsy?

It wouldn't, Grade decided. Dental emergencies happened, and people didn't always deal with them immediately for one reason or another. If Grade planned to drop the body at the bottom of the house's grand staircase, that would be different.

The dead woman obviously cared about her appearance. Someone like that wouldn't go to a party with a missing tooth.

A run to Whole Foods, though? Maybe.

Not that there *was* a Whole Foods in Sweeny, Grade thought sourly as he caught up with himself. He'd have to go to Louisville for that.

Plastic crinkled as Grade stood up and stepped back. He picked up the tags of tape that held it down at the corners and pulled it around the corpse. Not too tight, but he made sure every loose seam was sealed up. He left one flap open, just over her stomach.

The mental timer he'd set when he'd taken the job nudged the back of his brain. Two-thirds through the time he'd allocated himself for this stage… and with half the job left to do, that math didn't work.

It was going to have to.

He'd already soaked up most of the blood, stained cloths rolled up and tied in vacuum-pack bags, and doused the stained areas of the floor with bleach solution. It had lifted the tacky scabs of half-dried blood and diluted the wine down to rosé. The mix of alcohol and chlorine hung in the air, strong enough to catch in Grade's chest as he breathed it in.

Might be an idea to dilute it a bit more next time. Grade pulled his mask up over his mouth and nose, the stiff bridge of it a familiar itch across the bridge of his nose, and got down on his knees. He scrubbed up the sludgy mixture, dumped the sodden cloths in a bag, and did it again with new ones. The need to hurry up gnawed at the back of Grade's brain as he worked, a dull, nervy prod that settled in the hinges of his jaw like pressure.

He ignored it.

Grade had been intimidated by Russian gangsters and drug kingpins—well, third or fourth in the line of succession at least. If they'd not been able to push him into doing slipshod work, his own brain wasn't going to sabotage him now.

Once the floor was clean, Grade sprayed it down again and left the bleach to soak into the grout. At least it was tiled and not carpeted. There had been a rug crumpled up under the dead man, but Grade had cut it into strips to get rid of later. He dragged his kit bag over the damp floor to the floor-to-ceiling wine racks that decorated one wall of the cellar.

The door into the cellar opened, and a second later Harry came down the stairs, coat draped over one arm. He had remembered to pull the pair of blue paper bootees Grade had given him over his boots. The tail end of a cashmere scarf trailed down the steps after him. He had the grace to at least try and look sorry he'd missed most of the job.

"Turns out the coat check guy is also the weed hookup guy," he explained. "Half the guests and most of the staff were going in and out. I had to hang back and wait for a lull in business before I went in."

Grade pushed his hair away from his forehead with the back of his wrist. "Christ. This town's getting worse," he said. "Now the drug dealers need a side hustle?"

Harry just shook his head and made a long leg to skip over the last, still bloody step.

"Weed's a seasonal market round here," he said. "Particularly for a small-business owner. He probably makes bank when the hunters are in town. What do you want me to do with these?"

He waved his armful of outerwear. Grade pointed at the bodies. "Put them over there."

Harry looked and pulled a face. "Ah, man, they look like spring rolls. That's just wrong." He skirted the edge of the bleach and headed over to the corner. "I don't know how you're not a vegetarian."

"I never get that," Grade said.

"What?"

"You break people's fingers for a living—"

"That's not all I do," Harry protested. He hesitated for a second and then set the stuff down on the floor next to the bodies. "Don't diminish my role in the organization. I'm a vital cog in the machine."

"Dory said that, last week at the Slap, you literally broke the manager's fingers by smashing them in his desk drawer."

"Caught him with them in the till," Harry said. "And if I ever need to look for a new job, that's going on my resume as being a loss-prevention officer."

"My point," Grade said as he started to wipe the sticky mix of baking soda and toothpaste off the wine racks, "is that violence doesn't bother you."

Harry turned his mouth down at the corners in a facial shrug. "I wouldn't say that. I don't enjoy it," he said. "It's just part of the job, and not like it comes as a surprise to any of them. If you get into this line of work, you know that a slap on the wrist is going to leave you in a cast, not with a performance-improvement plan."

"But you get squeamish over some dead people that don't care what I do with them?"

"Yeah," Harry said, "I do. People like pork, but no one wants to see the sausage being made."

"Good news for you, then," Grade said as he wiped the last shelf down. The cloth was thick with paste, and the cleaned wood

looked rich, as well as cinnamon-scented. He used to grab his
own toothpaste on the way out to a job and left everything minty
fresh. Then he'd had the idea to grab the cinnamon stuff. He'd no
clue why anyone wanted to brush their teeth with it, but the
smell was more… woody. "We're not making sausage tonight.
Everyone stays in one piece."

Harry puffed out both cheeks with a relieved sigh. "Great.
That means I don't have to worry about God striking me down
when I take my grandma to church on Sunday. So what are we
doing?"

Grade stuck the paste-stiff cloth in his back pocket and
started to slot the bottles of wine back into place. He'd left the
dust and cobwebs undisturbed as much as possible—wine
collectors liked the bottles to look old; it was part of the
aesthetic—and the ones he'd needed to wipe blood off were set
out on a nearby table as if ready for a tasting.

"I guess you could say," he said, as he paused with a bottle
of Chateau Margaux hefted in one hand, "we're going to dress
the pig up and put on a show?"

Harry grimaced. "OK, found a way to make it worse," he
said. He tilted his head toward the two bodies. "How do we get
Mr. and Mrs. Spring Roll out of here?"

There was a spot of blood on the cork of the wine. Grade
should have caught that on the first go-over. He sighed and stuck
the bottle between his knees as he worked the cork out.

"Thirsty?" Harry asked.

Grade ignored that. "Go upstairs and see if you can find two
big rugs. Six foot wide at least."

For some reason, Harry looked disappointed. "Seriously?" he
said. "That's a bit old school, isn't it?"

Grade worked the cork free, caught the spill-over on his sleeve, and held the bottle out to Harry.

"Old school still works," he said. "But first, drink some of this."

Harry didn't need to be asked twice. He took a heavy, thirsty gulp and then grimaced as the taste hit.

"Fuck," he said. "That's sweet."

"That's about $200 worth of sweet," Grade told him as he took the bottle back. That was easier than trying to find someone discreet to empty a glassful of the stuff. He set it down on the table next to the rest. "Go get the rugs."

Harry wiped his mouth on his sleeve. "Two hundred bucks for a bottle of that?"

"No," Grade said. "For that drink."

Harry eyeballed the bottle for a moment and then shook his head. "I guess it's good to know I don't have expensive tastes," he said. "OK. So what do I do if I can't find two big rugs?"

Grade didn't know. He wasn't going to admit that, though.

"They've got wooden floors, and they invite people that wear their heels inside," he said. "They have rugs. Just find a couple. I need to see if I can track down some toenails."

DIRTY JOB

CHAPTER FOUR

CLAY LEFT THE Lexus parked in the back of the barn and drove with one hand on the Bentley's steering wheel and half an eye on the road as he typed Melanie Ledger's address into the text box.

1019 Eglandine Way.

Doglan.

The sudden squawk of a car horn jolted Clay's attention back to the road. He squinted into the glare of oncoming headlights and spun the wheel to veer the car back onto his side of the road. The pickup whose lane he'd drifted into just about scraped past without taking the mirror off the Bentley.

"Shit," Clay muttered as he steadied the wheel.

The leather slipped against his gloved palm, and...

...the wheels spun on the road as Clay hit the brakes. Ezra toppled back into his seat with a grunt of surprise, and Taylor Swift hit the chorus. Khalid's eyes were wide and wet as the lights caught him. He looked—

—heavy—

—guilty—

—dangerous—

Clay took a quick, ragged breath. He could taste the sand and gasoline on the back of his throat.

"Clay!" Ezra said. "Stop!"

He grabbed for the wheel and tried to wrestle it to the side. Clay stiff-armed him back onto his side of the car.

Fuck.

Clay tightened his hands around the wheel and stared at Khalid through the sand-blasted windshield. He—

No. Fuck that.

Clay white-knuckled his brain back into the here and now. The Bentley smelled like perfume and good leather, not stale sweat and cheap fucking liquor. The road stretched out ahead of him. Straight gray concrete dashed with bright white lines. No sign of any sand. No one caught in the low-slung beams of the Bentley as it roared forward.

The growl of the engine made Clay glance at the speedometer. He watched the needle ratchet up toward the red as he bit his lower lip. Adrenaline kicked his heart rate up and made his throat tighten with anticipation.

Sex, violence, and fast cars. Nothing better to blow the shadows of the past away. Clay kept his foot on the gas a moment longer as the needle quivered in the red and then pulled back.

The car held its speed for a few seconds, and then it started to drop off. As the Bentley slowed down, Clay looked back at the phone to check the message.

"Shit," he muttered and corrected himself.

EglanTine, he tapped in. Three dots flickered at the bottom of the app as Grade started to reply. Clay hung on to see what he had to say. His eyes flicked from the phone, held loosely in his free hand, to the road and back again. Finally the gray speech bubble popped up on the screen.

Dogleg? Just when I thought this job couldn't get any better.

Clay laughed and reached over to drop the phone onto the passenger seat. It always amused him that as much as Grade hated Sweeny, he still hated Doglan more on principle.

Grade pulled his other glove on with his teeth and dropped the driver's side window, the motor almost silent as the glass slid into the door. He hung his arm out, tapped his fingers on the metal side of the car, and glanced sporadically at the dial to keep his speed to the reasonable side of too fast.

§

It was a nice house.

Not exactly Circuit Court Judge nice, but still pretty nice.

1019 Eglantine Way was a two-story farmhouse-style house set back from the sidewalk on a fair-sized plot of land. The grass was mowed, the flower beds weeded, and it looked exactly the same as a dozen other houses on this stretch of road.

Grade's dirty white van looked out of place parked outside. The first thing that any suspicious neighbor would clock when they looked through their curtains.

Clay hesitated for a second as he flexed his hands around the steering wheel. This would be a hell of a way to find out Grade was bad at his job. But what the hell, he decided, he'd always expected to go to jail for something. He put the window up as he rolled the Bentley along the road until he could pull up onto the drive.

There'd been a garage opener tucked into Melanie's purse, Clay had found it when he'd hunted through for her ID, but he didn't need to hunt it back out. As he pulled up to the doors, the scratches and dents picked out in the headlights, they started to roll up automatically. Clay was briefly impressed, but on second thought, there were some obvious fucking drawbacks.

While he waited for the doors to open all the way, he reached over to check his phone.

There was a one-word text from Grade that just said *here.*
He called.

"I'm outside," he said when the ringtone cut out. "What now?"

"Leave the car in the garage," Grade said. "Hold on… No, not that. Go check her bedroom for any jewelry. Yeah, Clay, sorry about that. Meet us inside."

He hung up.

Clay hitched his hip and tucked the phone into his back pocket. He didn't plan to bring it up—when someone lived in a glass house of badly repressed trauma, they shouldn't throw stones—but sometimes he wondered which Grade was the mask. The one that was dryly funny and full of prickly self-regard about how smart he was or the quietly efficient butcher whose emotional range was a flat line?

Both of them turned Clay on, so it wasn't a problem for him. He just wondered. He drove into the garage and pulled up to the boxes stacked against the back wall of the space.

A glance in the mirror and a brief pause confirmed that the door came down on its own as well—once whatever sensor it used was satisfied it wasn't going to clip something. Clay waited until it clunked into place against the floor and then got out of the car. He shifted the front seat back to where it had been when he'd gotten in, dropped the steering wheel, and grabbed Melanie's bag off the front seat. It dangled from his hand as he headed into the house.

The lights were on inside, illuminating the long stretches of honey-gold wood and the soft green-painted walls. Clay paused in the hallway. Before he had to try and track them down, Grade leaned out of the kitchen.

"Down here," he said softly.

Clay glanced into a room as he walked past. The books had been pulled off shelves and scattered on the floor, cushions ripped open and gutted of their stuff. A handful of drawers had been pulled out of the cupboards and upended on the floor.

"Not much of a housekeeper, was she," Clay said dryly as he stepped into the kitchen.

Grade snorted as he pulled open a cutlery drawer and got out a knife. He held it like he'd never cut anything in his life, not even a sandwich. Clay bit the inside of his lip as he resisted the urge to correct his form.

"Melanie Ledger is going to look like she died after interrupting a robbery at her house," Grade said.

He stabbed the knife into the wooden counter. It was a nice knife too, German from the heavy curved blade. Clay made a mental note not to let Grade ever cook at his house.

For one thing, he thought tartly, that was definitely the point that fuck buddy hopped straight to boyfriend.

"I thought the whole point was low-key?" he said. "No scandal. Natural causes."

Grade stopped what he was doing and squinted at him. "The man was beaten to death with a wine bottle. What am I supposed to pretend that was, an attack by an alcoholic bear?"

There was a snort from behind Clay. He turned to look at Harry, who had a handful of gold chains in one hand and a silver pleather jacket in the crook of his elbow.

"What? It was funny," Harry said. "And only a bit creepy."

"Shut up," Clay told him.

Grade turned his back as he opened some cabinets and swept the contents out. Spices hit the counter and spilled open, the smell of garlic and cumin strong enough to make Clay's nose itch.

"If the house had been more isolated, I could have just staged a fall," Grade said. "But someone is going to see the van outside or two men hauling a rug into the house at—"

He stopped to look for a clock. Harry checked the one he had clutched in his hand and said, "Nearly midnight."

"And that means it wasn't natural causes, and if nothing was taken, it wasn't a robbery either," Grade said. He fastidiously brushed garlic powder from his gloved hands. "Only fourteen percent of burglaries are solved. The stats for murder are much more impressive."

Clay held up his hands. "It was just an observation," he said. "This shitshow is all yours. I cause problems; I don't fix 'em."

For a second Grade looked flustered as he glanced at Clay's hands, still in close-fitting leather gloves. He flushed a little, just around the ears, and had to clear his throat before he could push on.

"Good to know," Grade said.

"Didn't skip those grades in school for being observant, huh?" Clay said. He shrugged when Grade scowled at him. "Not like I was hiding it."

Harry dumped two handfuls of jewelry into a pillowcase.

"Yeah. He can get references," he said. The back of an earring caught in his glove and ripped the latex. "Shit."

Grade pulled another pair out of a pocket and held them out, wrinkled and blue as they dangled from his fingers.

"You're about to have a new experience, then," he said. "Help us move the body into the hall."

"Where is she?"

They'd left her in the study.

"You take the feet," Grade said as he lifted books off the floor and relocated them onto the dead woman's desk. "Harry, get the head."

"Couldn't you have waited to trash in here until you were done?" Grade asked.

Harry straddled one end of the plastic-wrapped corpse and bent from the knees as he got ready to lift her. "It was like this when we got here," he said. "I thought the place had already been turned over."

"Wrong end," Grade told him absently as he moved a brown leather kitchen chair out of their way, one hand on the files stacked on it to keep them in place.

"Does it matter?"

"Yes," Grade said.

It didn't. Clay could tell when Grade was just being a dick for the sake of it. They could fight about that later, when they weren't under a deadline. Right now, he just gestured at Harry for them to swap places.

"What about the other one?" Clay asked. "Franklin."

Grade stopped what he was doing and looked annoyed. That was Clay being a petty bastard back at him. Clay knew Grade didn't like to think of corpses as people; it made it easier to keep a professional distance.

"How invested was the client in them not being found together?" Grade asked.

"Like my first boyfriend's dad about me," Clay said. "Very."

Grade sighed. "Then we'll need to go back and get the Lexus." He pulled his sleeve back and frowned at his watch. His lips moved slightly as he counted off the hours. "I'll have to cut it close, but there should be time. Well, there will be if we get on with it here."

He nodded pointedly to the body.

"On the count of three," Clay told Harry as they both bent down and grabbed the body. "One. Two. And… up."

Clay grunted as he took the weight. Alive, it wouldn't have been a problem, but dead people were awkward bastards. He hung on as he backed out of the room and into the hall. He started to turn as he made it over the threshold.

"Other way," Grade said as he waved his hand toward the kitchen. "Feet need to go up the stairs."

The plastic made it hard to keep a good grip on the corpse. Clay clenched his teeth and hung on to it as he shifted direction. He backed up until Harry levered the dead body out through the door.

"Reminds me of Ezra's wedding," Clay said as he waited for Harry to adjust his grip.

Harry snorted as he glanced over his shoulder and then edged backward toward the front door.

"Reminds me of his divorce," he said.

"Don't drop it," Grade instructed as they got to the foot of the stairs. Clay took a couple of steps up, cautiously and backward, as Harry lowered the other end of the body to the floor. "Set it down gently."

Clay raised his eyebrows at Harry, who laughed. "OK. You win," he said. "Wedding."

Grade stepped around Harry and crouched next to the body. He used a pocket knife to cut neatly through the outer layer of plastic and tape. Then he peeled the rest away like a shell until they could see the dead woman again.

"Lift her up," he said.

They did, and he dragged the cut-up sheets out from under her. He folded them fastidiously and set them aside as they lowered her back down.

"So how the fuck does Ezra know Judge Parker, anyhow?" Harry asked as he backed away. "Doesn't seem like a match made in heaven."

Clay leaned on the banister and answered absently while he watched Grade work. "Her grandson and Ally go to ballet class together."

Grade positioned the woman's body impersonally. He hung the shoe at the exact, precarious angle off her toes. Or close enough to fool Clay.

"What? Seriously?" Harry asked.

"Sure," Clay said as he looked up at Harry. He held it for a second and then snorted. "Of course they fucking don't. The Catfish Mafia have their hooks into Judge Parker, and they didn't want her big announcement to go ahead without reminding her of that fact."

Harry snorted as he looked down at the dead woman, her hair flicked out so it fanned around her face.

"That ain't gonna slip her mind for a while," he said. "Not after they got this mess cleaned up for her."

Yeah. Things were a bit more complicated than that, of course, but… Yeah.

"She'll be so far in someone's pocket that she could scratch his balls," Clay said as he pushed himself up straight. He cracked his neck and felt the release of pressure all the way up into the back of his head. "Is that it, Grade? I've still got a shit party to attend."

Grade shook a sliver of something pink out of a baggie onto the stairs. It was probably better not to ask what.

"I'm nearly done here," he said as he scrambled to his feet. "But I'll need to get the Lexus before you go back."

Clay nodded. He'd expected that. "It's waiting for you. Don't say I never give you anything good."

That made Grade's detached composure slip as he grinned, quick and crookedly wicked.

"Does that mean you're reneging on the other thing you were going to give me?" he asked.

Clay braced his hands on both railings and boosted himself up so he could swing himself over the dead woman. He hit his mark in the hallway and nudged his shoulder against Grade on the way by.

"You mean my cock?" he said as he leaned in closer to Grade's ear. He could smell unexpectedly floral shampoo under the bleach and antiseptic scent that clung to Grade like aftershave. "Don't worry. I'll even keep the suit on."

The tops of Grade's ears went pink as if someone had pinched them as he took a ragged breath. "Gloves too," he said.

Clay paused for a second as his muscles tightened with the urge to grab Grade by the collar and just shove him back against the wall. He could almost feel Grade's throat under his hand, the way it moved when he swallowed and tilted his head back to be kissed...

It had been a while. Not deliberately; things had just kept getting in the way. A problem with distribution a few towns over that the Catfish Mob expected sorted out as the price of doing business. Some biker's old lady had run down a cop and needed her car deep cleaned before the cops impounded it.

Before he could do anything, Harry cleared his throat.

"I'm going to be honest," he said. "You guys make a cute couple, but not sure that will help if we get caught."

Grade stepped back from Clay, suddenly awkward. "We're not a couple," he said. "We just fuck."

Clay frowned.

It was close enough to what Clay had said earlier, so he didn't have reason to feel pissed off about it. Still was, though. It was lucky that he was jacked in the head and didn't have a "good reason" for half the stuff he felt. Or if you listened to his therapist—which he tried to avoid—none that he was willing to deal with.

"Yeah, well, that's worse," Harry said. "I'm not comfortable with the idea of telling my wife that is what ended up with me in jail."

"Don't worry," Grade said. "I wasn't going to ask you to join in."

"Sure, because 'me and the corpse just watched' sounds better," Harry said. "That's not going to end up in a meme somewhere."

Grade ducked around Clay and headed back into the kitchen. "No one is going to get caught tonight," he said. "It takes, on average, forty minutes for the local deputies to respond to a call about a household burglary. We're still within our window."

He disappeared through the door. When he came out a second later, he had a mini-cooler in one hand.

"Hungry?" Clay asked.

It started out sarcastic, but now he thought about it, he could eat. A couple of crackers and a single shrimp was not a meal. He still couldn't believe Charity had made a big do like that and not even sprung for a tray of devilled eggs or something.

Grade looked confused for a moment and then hefted the cooler. "Oh, this?" he said. "No, this is the last touch, and then we can go. Someone lift her head?"

He didn't nominate anyone for the job, and neither Clay nor Harry jumped in to do the needful. Clay supposed he could just tell Harry to do it, but that would make him look squeamish. He'd never live it down.

"How far up?" he asked as he knelt next to the dead woman on the floor.

Clay cupped both hands around her head. It felt weird. He'd killed people before. Some of it had been in the army and some for Ezra, and he'd probably have to add the Catfish Mob to that list sooner or later. That didn't bother him.

Liar, liar. Pants on fire. The old rhyme skittered through his head on a manic singsong. He worked his jaw from one side to the other and ignored it.

This—the weight of the woman's head, the slack, waxy slide of her face as she stared up—bothered him. But fuck that too, and the part of his brain that was nudging at him with the "why." He didn't need to know. In fact, probably better he didn't. In Clay's experience, men with complicated internal lives did not thrive in his line of work.

"Not like that. Your feet are in the way," Grade said. He gestured with his free hand. "Stand over her."

Clay rolled his eyes but did as he was told. He straddled her shoulders and cupped the back of her neck with one hand as Grade knelt where Clay had been a second ago. He opened the cooler and pulled out a blood bag.

"What the fuck?" Clay said. "Where did you get that? Is that yours?"

"What? No." Grade swept up the dead woman's hair in one hand to keep it out of the way as he emptied about half the bag onto the waxed wooden floorboards. "Maybe it didn't come up in Doing Crime 101, but don't leave your DNA at a crime scene."

"So where did you get it?"

"It's her blood. I extracted it back at the original scene." Grade added another few drips to the puddle and then tied off the bag. It went back in the cooler. "You can set her head back down now. Gently."

"Damn," Clay deadpanned. He lowered the dead woman's head. It squelched softly as it settled into the small pool of blood. "I was going to try and spike it like a football."

Grade snorted and snapped the lid of the cooler shut.

"That's it," he said. "Now we just have to wait and see what ends up in the news."

"Let's get out of here, then," Clay said. He straightened up, stepped away from the dead woman, and offered Grade a gloved hand up. "Just in case the traffic is good tonight."

Harry glanced between them and then down at the dead woman.

"Really?" he said skeptically. "That's it? No drugs or chemicals? No hacking into her phone to post deceptive updates on Facebook or something?"

"That is touching far too many things," Grade said. "You don't want to give whoever is on the case too many opportunities to do a good job."

He loped off to grab the bags from the kitchen. There was visibly more urgency to his pace than there had been when they arrived.

Harry scratched his head.

"What if it doesn't work?" he said. "What if they don't buy it?"

Grade came back out, bags slung over his shoulders. He shrugged and nearly dislodged his backpack as it slid down his arm.

"To start with, I don't offer a guarantee, and I have a no-refund policy," he said as he hitched the strap back up into place. "But hopefully the local cops will prove to be just as useless now as they were when my dad died."

Clay took one of the bags off him and dangled it from his hand.

"Odds are in our favor," he said. "Me and Ezra aren't exactly criminal geniuses, and the sheriff has never made anything stick."

Harry snorted. "You remember I used to be a cop, right?"

"It's not slipped my mind."

Harry glared at him for a moment, then muttered under his breath as he got a balaclava out of his pocket and pulled it down over his face. It went on crooked, and he had to yank at the seams to get both eyeholes in the right place.

"Here," Grade said. He held out another black mask. "I brought a spare."

Clay gave the thing an aggrieved look. It wasn't like he'd never worn one before, and that was the point. He knew what the wool and sweat would do to his hair. He'd worn enough of them when he was a SEAL.

But the choice was bad hair or a bad identikit of him on the news as the anchor asked, "Have you seen this man?" So…

He took it and pulled it on. Then he gestured at the door.

"Time to go," he said. "Before luck runs out."

Harry didn't need to be told twice. He ducked out through the front door and loped toward the van. Clay started to follow him and then realized that Grade wasn't at his heels. He turned back just in time to see Grade backtrack down the hall.

"What happened to 'that's it'?" he asked.

"I forgot something," Grade said. He waved his hand dismissively. "Go on. I'll meet you at the van."

Clay glared at Grade's back as he hesitated in the doorway. He did a quick mental calculation, and it turned out Grade's ass was not worth jail.

"Idiot," he muttered as he ducked out and ran for the van.

Harry was in the driver's seat, mask pulled up to his forehead. He gave Clay a curious look.

"Where's Grade?"

Clay paused in the middle of chucking the bag into the van. He squinted at Harry for a moment and then rolled his eyes.

"Guess."

The bags went in, and he walked around the van to climb into the passenger seat.

"So, what?" Harry asked. "We just wait on him?"

"No," Clay said. He pulled the mask off and tossed it onto the floor. "Either he hits his mark or he makes his own way."

"What happened to 'No Man Left Behind'?" Harry asked as he turned the keys in the ignition.

"That's the Marines," Clay said. "Let's go."

The van engine rumbled to life. Harry dragged his seatbelt over his chest and clicked it into place. He checked the mirrors and grabbed the stick to shift out of park.

Grade loped out of the front door of the house, laptop under one arm and backpack bouncing on his back, and headed for the van. The engine noise revved up as Harry shifted gears and spun the wheel around, ready to peel out.

It didn't look like Grade was going to make it. Fuck sake. Clay reached out and grabbed Harry's wrist.

"Wait," he said.

"You said to—"

"Shut up," Clay told him.

Grade scrambled into the back of the van and slammed the doors behind him.

"Now go," Clay said as he relaxed his grip.

Harry yanked the wheel, hit the gas, and peeled away from the curb. Unsecured bags slid around the back and bounced off the walls as they tore down the road. Grade cursed as he staggered and nearly fell onto the body still bungeed to the floor.

As they left the neighborhood and the last neat farmhouse-style houses were replaced with shuttered shop fronts and pockmarked forecourts, Clay saw two of the sheriff department's patrol cars turn onto the road behind them.

"Thirty minutes," Grade said mildly as he hung on to the back of Clay's seat for balance. "Maybe they brought in an efficiency expert?"

CHAPTER FIVE

GRADE PULLED THE bat out of the back of the van. He hefted it in one hand and gave a short practice swing. Then he turned to look speculatively at Harry, who looked like he might not have spent every PE class since he was twelve on the bench.

"No," Harry said. He held up both hands and took a step back until his shoulders hit the side of the van. "I'm Catholic, and I don't want to have to explain this shit to the priest. Just get on with it."

Great.

Grade gripped the handle of the bat in both hands and looked down at the dead man. They were parked in a scenic cutout on the side of the road, the van nudged in closest while the Lexus had been left back on the verge. On the other side of the age-bleached wooden barriers, the side of the mountain dropped down precipitously into tree-covered thickets and rocky outcrops. The air smelled like damp rock and turkey shit.

When they'd gotten the dead man out of the back of the van, they'd cut him out of the plastic. He was laid out face-up on the cracked concrete and discarded wrappers. Despite Grade's best efforts when he'd wrapped him, the plastic had creased the corpse's mouth together. The sallow lips were folded into something that was almost a smile.

Grade wasn't superstitious. Salt was for your fries, not to throw over your shoulder, and it didn't matter what day you cut your nails; if you were cutting them in Sweeny, then you weren't that lucky. That smug twist of a smile on the corpse's face still made the back of Grade's neck itch uncomfortably.

"Something wrong?" Harry asked. Out of the corner of Grade's eye he saw the other man pull the cuff of his jacket back to check his watch. "You said we needed to drop the car off by—"

"I know," Grade said. He shook off the queasy disquiet. "Just thinking of how I'd be spending Friday night if I was still in LA."

Harry chuckled, the sound unexpectedly clear against the still night air. "What?" he mocked. "You'd be out partying with movie stars?"

Once. Well, CW actors… and one of them had been dead. The party had been over by that point.

"Most nights it would have been something like this," Grade admitted. He set the end of the bat on the ground and pulled his earphones out of his pocket. They were already linked to his phone, and the tinny notes of Doja Cat's little single filtered out. "The difference is, it was in LA."

He plugged the earphones in, filling his head with noise, and swung the bat. The end of it connected with the side of the dead man's head, right on the indent that a wine bottle had already left there. Grade felt the impact up into his elbows, and the man's head jolted to the side.

Harry watched for a while. Then he grimaced and went to stand at the barrier so he could peer down over the moonlit town. Grade could have told him that wouldn't work. He lined up the bat with the dead man's caved-in clavicle. It was the noises that got most people.

§

"Gotta tell you," Harry said, "I've had better nights."

Blood dripped sluggishly off the end of the bat as Grade sprayed it with bleach. He wiped it down and stashed it back inside the van. There was a donation bin on the way back into Sweeny. He'd drop it in there. After a week in the hands of a small child in Sweeny, any forensic evidence on it would be seriously compromised.

"Maybe you should ask Ezra for a bonus," Grade said.

Harry laughed at that. Then he jerked his thumb toward the corpse.

"So now we just, what?" he said. "Toss him over the edge, and that's it?"

"More or less," Grade said. "After that, all I need you to do is get the Lexus to a good chop shop. I'll get rid of the rest of the evidence."

"I can do that," Harry offered. "You take the Lexus, and maybe you'll make that date with Clay."

Grade hesitated long enough that Harry snorted at him, "You don't work well with others, do you?"

"That's what my report cards said," Grade said.

Although the "date" thing had given him pause too. People dated when they planned to hang around a while. But "no strings sex appointment" didn't exactly flow in conversation, he supposed.

Grade motioned for Harry to follow him and then walked over to the corpse. Dead bodies didn't actively bleed, but anyone who'd slapped down a fresh ribeye on a counter could tell you that they did splatter. Resculpting the injuries had left a bit of a mess. Grade avoided the splatter as he walked forward and grabbed the man's arms while Harry got his feet.

"It already looks bad that my work history went from high profile gigs in LA to scrubbing out dive bar bathrooms after some man got shot taking a piss—"

They hoisted the dead man off the ground.

"I mean, it was the bagman for the Catfish Mafia," Harry said. The corpse swung between them as they walked to the rails. "Not just some trucker who got shanked for his wallet. Leave out the bit where you lost the body, and that's not too bad."

Grade winced at *that* reminder. He nodded to Harry to lift, and they swung the dead man up and over the rail.

"I'm pretty sure some Bratva boss in LA is going to think the Catfish Mafia is a hot new food truck. On three. One. Two."

They let go.

The corpse hit the scree on the other side and lay for a moment. Grade thought he was going to have to get a stick and poke him into the drop. Then gravity did its work and dragged him over the edge.

Grade tucked his hands into his pockets, the latex catching on the fabric, and watched as the body tumbled down the cliff. It bounced off rocks and trees until it finally landed in the interlocked branches of two scrawny oak trees. The body swung there, one arm and leg dangling awkwardly as the trees bent but didn't break under the weight.

"Shit," Harry said. "Do we need to climb down and shake it loose?"

"No. Leave it," Grade said. It wasn't ideal. He'd hoped the body wouldn't be found for a few days. However, the longer someone messed around with a scene, the more likely they were to make a mistake. "And that's why I prefer to work alone. The only thing about my stay in Kentucky that LA criminals will find impressive is if none of my clients get caught. So I don't want to give anyone else the opportunity to make a mistake I wouldn't."

He stepped back and scuffed the sole of his sneaker over the concrete, smearing the blood down to another dark, indistinct stain.

Harry narrowed his eyes at him. "Is that a nice way to say that you think I'm an idiot?"

Grade stopped what he was doing to look at him.

"No," he said. "That would be a dumb thing to tell a professionally violent man on a lonely road."

Harry gave him that with a shrug. "Fair enough. So what did you mean?"

"That if they want to get rid of a dead body, they call me," Grade said. He shrugged, gave the ground one last scuff, and headed back to the van. "And if they want to make one, then they call you."

"They'd call Clay first," Harry said.

It felt like a warning. Grade didn't need one. He knew what he was getting with Clay. He headed back to the van and fished the keys to the Lexus out of the central console.

"It doesn't matter what happens to the car," he said. "As long as they don't drop you in it."

He tossed the keys. Harry caught them out of the air.

"They won't," he said. "If they aren't scared of Ezra, they are of Fisher and his crew. Can I ask you something?"

That was the sort of question they usually asked just before they wanted to know something about Grade's life that was none of their business. It was like they thought they could grandfather in their nosiness as long as they started with being polite.

"What?" Grade asked anyhow.

Harry jangled the keys idly in one hand. "Do you *really* have a resume?" he asked.

§

The rugs were thick and expensive, the pile short but so dense it felt like velvet. Grade got them out of the van with a grunt, one after the other, and dragged them over the hard-packed dirt and into the old machine shop.

No one came out to the old mining camp on the outskirts of Sweeny. It wasn't well-preserved enough to be historical or creepy enough to interest TikTok vloggers. And it was way too out of town to be worth the trip for the local teenagers. Other than Grade, the last person who'd been out here had been the guy who'd towed the old storage unit all the way from Lexington for him.

It was amazing the places you could get people to deliver things to, as long as you paid on time and weren't overtly weird.

He laid the rugs out on the floor and went into the storage container to get the shears to cut them up. It took twenty minutes, and by the end his hands ached and he had a pile of shedding carpet strips. He tossed them into the waiting drums, on top of his shoes and the rest of the stuff he'd taken from the scene to get rid of.

Back in LA, he knew a few other people who did what he did. Some of them dumped everything in water, the murkier and more pissed-in the better, while others went with acid or chemicals. They all had their pros and cons. Grade preferred fire.

He grabbed the industrial-sized bottle of paint thinner, soaked the shredded rug thoroughly, and then struck a match. It flickered dimly under the fluorescent lighting he'd strung up, the heat of it building as it burned down toward his fingers, and then tossed it into the drum. The accelerant caught hungrily, and flames scorched the inside of the drum. Grade grabbed a pole, hooked out a strip of flaming wool, and tossed it into the second drum.

Grade left them to burn while he unloaded the bags of stolen goods they'd taken from the woman's house. He dumped them in the corner of the shop. They were unfinished business. Or at least undecided.

In LA, he had the contacts to drop the haul into the local black market. Give it a week and the cops would find flagged items as they turned up in pawn shops or on the fingers of some petty crook's mom. It made it look like a real burglary.

It would be harder to pull that off in Sweeny. Possible— Grade could pull in a few favors, ask for some names, hit up any of his dad's old associates who weren't in jail or the ground—but it would put him out there more than he was comfortable with. Too many opportunities for the cops to do their job right.

The risk probably wasn't worth the reward—and why he'd let Harry handle the Lexus, which he was starting to regret—but he didn't have to decide just yet.

Grade cleaned the inside of the van out quickly while the rugs burned. One thing about his new transport, it was quicker to scrub down. It was just bare metal walls and floors. All it took was a quick spray of concentrated bleach and a few minutes of focused scrubbing and you were left with a feeling of accomplishment and a mild cough.

The flames in the drums had guttered down by the time he finished. Grade grabbed the pole again to poke at the remains in the bottom. There were still a few bits of backing, curled and charred but intact, so he emptied the rest of the paint thinner in. It made the embers smoke; then the fumes caught and the flames belched up out of the metal. High enough that the heat stung Grade's wrists.

He pulled back and hissed softly, shaking his hands to shed the sting.

While they burned down, he grabbed the bags of stolen goods and hauled them outside. He lugged them through the woods until he reached the old, rusted manhole cover half-buried under dirt and leaves. Grade kicked them out of the way and bent down to hook his fingers into the pick hole. The fit wasn't tight, so it was easy enough to lift and drag out of the way.

Whatever had been down there had mostly dried out. From the smell, Grade assumed it had been a sewage tank. The layer of mulch down on the bottom and the stench were enough to dissuade casual interest.

Professional interest would be more thorough—but they'd have a hard time tying Grade to the location in any concrete way.

He knotted the bags together and dropped them into the hole. They hit the bottom with a squelch and a muted thud. Grade pulled the manhole cover back over and dropped it into place. He threw some rocks and dirt over it and then headed back to the shop.

The fires had guttered down into hot ashes when he stepped back in under the rotted-through roof. Grade could feel the heat from the metal against his legs. He grabbed two containers of water and poured them into the drums. Steam replaced smoke, dry and acrid. Once it sizzled out, he went and got the five liter bottles of acid wash and upended them. It was still hot enough to make the liquid bubble as it heated up, but that wouldn't do it any harm.

Well...

Grade lifted the bottle to squint at the label. Or at what was left of it, the paper stained and tattered. It wasn't easy to read, so… probably wouldn't do any harm. If it did, Grade didn't plan to be here to deal with it.

He grabbed the empty bottles and carried them over to chuck them into the back of the van with the cleaned-up bat. Then he checked his phone to see if there was any message from Harry about the Lexus.

Nothing.

Grade could *feel* his stress levels ratchet up a notch. The fact he couldn't do anything about it just made him feel more anxious, and he'd already been running hotter than normal on his nerves. The rationale that Clay had sold him on about how this was subcontracting, not breaking his rule about amateurs, felt thinner every time he thought about it.

He slammed the van doors shut.

Fuck it.

He'd not been sure whether he was going to go to Clay's tonight or not. It had gone from being too late for a hookup to too early for one. Plus, the idea that their no-strings thing might be an actual *thing* made Grade edgy enough that he wanted to give the whole concept a wide berth for a while.

Just long enough to prove that he didn't care about whatever he had with Clay.

Except he was too amped up to go back to his mom's house and deal with his family. It felt claustrophobic just standing in one place, like his skin was a size too small. Never mind being stuck in a kitchen while his mom cooked eggs—badly—and made veiled suggestions about him getting a proper job.

Staying in town.

Meeting a *nice* boy.

And at this point the hints were about as veiled as the dancers on stage with Dory at the Choke. Grade didn't know what conversation pasties looked like, and he didn't want to find out over burned scrambled eggs.

The best way to burn off nervous energy was sex, at least it was for Grade, and he could prove he didn't care some other time. When it was convenient.

It wouldn't be hard. Grade had done it to lots of people over the years when it felt like they might get too close. He doubted Clay would be any different.

People, in general, weren't.

Grade left the chemicals to work on the rugs as he climbed up into the driver's seat. The engine grumbled to life, but he left the lights off as he bumped out of the old building and along the rutted, broken-up road. The bat and bottles rattled around in the back with each pothole he hit on his way down to the highway.

He stopped on the way to toss the bat into the charity collection and the bottles into recycling. Business before pleasure.

§

Clay opened the front door.

He'd not changed out of the suit or rolled his sleeves down. The sketchy red-and-black lines of his ink looked very dark in the last of the moonlight. Clay leaned against the doorframe, arms folded and one leg crossed in front of the other. His feet were bare.

Grade's breath caught in the back of his throat, suddenly dry and scratchy.

"I wasn't sure you'd still be up," he said.

Clay looked amused as he tilted his head to the side. The throb of industrial music leaked out of the house from behind him. It was a good thing his neighbors were a fair distance away. "If I was a fan of early nights," he said, "I wouldn't take the sort of shit I take."

That was the other reason to be grateful this thing wasn't anything real. Otherwise Grade couldn't have just ignored that. Where they stood right now, he could. And did.

"You going to invite me in?" he asked. "Or not?"

Clay glanced over his shoulder and hesitated for a beat. Then he shrugged and stepped to the side.

"What the hell, the hookers should have made themselves scarce by now," he said and gestured grandly with one arm. "Mi casa es su casa."

"If that was true," Grade said, "you'd do your recycling."

Clay laughed and headed back into the house, the door left open behind him.

"Considering the number of laws you break," he tossed over his shoulder, "you worry an awful lot about following the rules."

Grade stepped over the threshold and closed the door behind him.

"You know how many people end up in prison for a felony *because* the cops pulled them over for a bald tire and then found other evidence?" Grade asked.

Clay turned away and kept walking backward. "One," he said. He was right. That was annoying. Clay grinned smugly at Grade. "I'm right, aren't I?"

"Maybe," Grade said sourly. "But I'm not going to make it two."

Clay laughed at him and turned back around. There was a bottle of bourbon and a half-full glass on the coffee table, close enough to the speakers to make the liquid ripple. Clay grabbed another tumbler from the drinks cabinet and splashed a shot into it.

"How'd the cleanup go?" he asked as he held the glass out to Grade. He raised an eyebrow. "Everything done and dusted? No loose ends?"

The urge to check his phone—in case a message had come in from Harry in the last minute—made Grade's fingers twitch.

"Nothing that worrying about it will fix," Grade said as he stepped forward and ignored the glass. He grabbed the front of Clay's shirt and pulled him into a hard bourbon-sweet kiss, the flavor of it chewed off Clay's mouth. Before Clay could respond in kind, Grade pulled back just enough to ask against the damp seam of Clay's lips, "So why don't you take my mind off it?"

CHAPTER SIX

CLAY DIDN'T MAKE plans.

In his experience that was just a hand-delivered invitation to the universe to fuck them up. Bad luck, assholes. A month in a military hospital getting dead flesh scraped off his arms three times a day by some doctor who skimped on the oxy. There was always something to throw a spanner in the works.

That said—Clay leaned back, his hands braced on the table behind him—he should have thought better of the music. It was still turned up loud enough he could feel it through his heels, all heavy bass and fast, insistent beats.

Fucking to this was going to leave him needing a new hip.

Clay glanced down at Grade—brown hair tangled from Clay's fingers and Clay's cock in his mouth—and idly wondered if he was getting too old for that joke to be funny. Probably not. Not yet, anyhow. His birthday wasn't for another three months.

Too jacked up…

Maybe.

He took a deep breath as Grade's tongue pushed up against the underside of his cock and felt the straps of scar tissue over his ribs pull painfully on the seams where it stitched into his skin. Clay sucked in a breath and waited for the sharp jab of pain to get watered down by the distraction of Grade's warm, eager mouth around him.

Grade pulled back and let Clay's cock slip out of his mouth. He looked up at Clay and then licked the tip of his cock with a slow, deliberate swipe of his tongue. Every fucking thing from Clay's nipples to his knees clenched into a knot. He swore between his teeth and grabbed a handful of hair to pull Grade's head back. His throat pulled tight, and... fuck, it had been a while. All the hickeys from last time had faded.

That could be fixed.

"Not going to finish the job?" he asked.

Grade ran his hands up Clay's thighs, and his thumbs skimmed along the inside seam of the tailored trousers until they framed the unzipped fly.

"That's what I was going to ask you," he said.

Clay made a low, amused sound in the back of his throat and tugged Grade's head back to a sharper angle. He watched Grade's eyes go dark and hungry, the green iris just a narrow line around the swollen pupils.

"Starting to think I should have told you to get lost," he said. "Kept the hookers."

Grade touched the tip of his tongue to his lower lip. The absent gesture briefly distracted Clay as he remembered what that tongue had just been doing. His balls pulled tight and tender, and he exhaled raggedly.

"That would be expensive," Grade said.

Clay snorted as he let go of Grade's hair. "You ain't exactly cheap."

A quick smile tucked the corners of Grade's mouth. His narrow frat-boy handsome face creased around the humor of it.

"You should see what I charge in LA," he said as he pushed himself to his feet. With Clay still slouched against the table and

Grade upright, he had to tilt his head back to look at him. "And I don't even throw in a free blow job."

Clay usually rolled his eyes when Grade talked about LA—whether it was how much better it was than Sweeny or how hard it was to get your foot *back* in the door—but that one startled a laugh out of him.

"The only thing in life that's free is those samples they give you in the supermarket," Clay said. He hooked his fingers into the waistband of Grade's sweats and pulled him in closer until he stood in the spread *V* of Clay's thighs. "Everything else you pay for eventually. One way or another."

He wasn't sure where he planned to go with that line of thought. It was a joke, the right smartass thing to say in response to Grade's jibe. Then he saw the flicker of flight-risk panic in Grade's pretty green eyes.

Clay knew the look. Usually it was because he'd just threatened to feed someone their own fucking fingers when he found out who'd shorted the cut. Apparently, with Grade, all he needed to suggest was that Grade might—one day—want something from Clay.

That kinda stung, Clay wasn't going to lie.

"The only thing I want is—"

Clay kissed him to shut him up, rough and impatient. He could taste the sticky saltiness of pre-come on Grade's lips as he deepened the kiss. It twisted the ache that had settled in his balls and itched down in the very base of his brain where all his addictions lived.

He slid his hand under Grade's sweatshirt and grazed it up his side, over the lean muscle along his ribs. The whimper that escaped Grade was soft, but Clay felt it against his tongue. He smirked and leaned back, away from Grade's brief attempt to chase the kiss.

"Shut up," Clay said as he wrapped his hand around Grade's throat, lightly at first as he watched Grade's face for his reaction. "I know what you want."

Grade tilted his head back and bit his lower lip. Color flushed high over his cheekbones and turned the tips of his ears pink.

"And yet you took the gloves off," he said.

Clay put his thumb under Grade's chin and tipped it back. "My hands got sweaty."

He could feel Grade's pulse flutter against his fingers as it sped up and the way his throat moved when he swallowed.

"You going to fuck me or not?" Grade asked.

Clay tightened his grip, just enough to make Grade gasp in reaction. He leaned in and kissed the soft skin under Grade's jawline, the scrape of his teeth not quite enough to leave a mark.

"Maybe you should ask nice," he rasped, the Southern accent he'd spent years rubbing the hick off thicker than he usually liked.

Grade wove his fingers through Clay's curls. "And what if I don't?"

Clay smiled against Grade's throat and then moved up to brush a kiss over the curve of his ear. "You still get fucked," he said. "It just won't be nice."

"Promises are cheap," Grade said, his voice tight. "Prove it."

There was probably, Clay mused as he lifted his head, an argument to be made that this was about his self-destructive streak. The music wasn't enough to live up to? He had to run his mouth too? Now he had to live up to the hype.

At this rate he was going to hit forty and fucking die of over-promising what his cock could do.

But what the hell. Everyone had to die of something. And if he didn't get killed on the job, with the amount of coke he did, his heart was the next most likely cause of death.

He pushed Grade back a couple of steps and let go of his throat.

"Take your clothes off," he said.

Grade stared at him for a heartbeat and then grabbed the bottom of his sweatshirt to drag it over his head. His arms got tangled in the sleeves, and he was flushed when he finally wrenched it off and tossed it aside. The sweatpants went next, stripped off along with his boxer briefs and left knotted around his ankles. His cock was flushed and ready, the skin pulled tight around the shaft.

"Your turn," he said.

Clay ran his finger around his collar to loosen it. "I think I'll keep it on."

"Good," Grade said as he kicked the clothes out of the way and stepped forward.

"I'm still going to make you say please," Clay said, then winked. "Sooner or later."

§

Clay pushed Grade up against the wall.

He bit a kiss into the nape of Grade's neck, as if he could taste the faint splatter of freckles, and slid his hand around to spread it across the taut flat of Grade's stomach. With clothes on, Grade looked lanky, all height and narrow shoulders. It was only when he was naked that you could see all the lean, wiry muscle he carried.

The music throbbed on in the background as Clay slid his hand down to Grade's hip. He felt Grade's breath hitch when he moved his hand on down past Grade's cock to stroke his lean, lightly-haired thigh.

Grade tilted his head back and grazed a kiss over the corner of Clay's mouth, along his jaw.

"I don't have all night," he said.

"Flirt," Clay said. He gripped the inside of Grade's thigh and pulled his legs apart. Muscle tightened under his grip as Grade shifted his weight. "Don't move."

Clay stepped back to admire the view of long, narrow back and nice ass while he pulled the packet of lube he'd bought earlier out of his pocket. He ripped a corner of it off between his teeth, the bubblegum sugary smell of it strong enough that he could almost *taste* it in his nose. It was clear and slippery as he squeezed it out over his fingers.

"You should get some ink." He reached out and ran one finger down Grade's spine, drawing a slippery line from his shoulder blades to the small of his back. Grade visibly shivered at the touch, and the muscles in his ass tightened. "I know a guy."

Grade looked around.

"Do you know how hard it is to find someone to tattoo a corpse?" he asked. "At short notice?"

Clay snorted and leaned in to grab a kiss from the corner of Grade's mouth.

"Sometimes you make being romantic hard." He slid his hand down over Grade's ass and pushed a slippery finger into him. Grade sucked in his breath in reaction, and his hands spread out against the wall. "Lucky we're just here to fuck, huh?"

Grade made a noise in the back of his throat that was probably agreement. When Clay pushed a second finger into him, he rose up onto his toes; the long lines of muscle over his ribs and down his flanks were pulled tight and defined under his skin. Clay caught his hip and pulled him back down. He scraped a series of wet, stubble-rough kisses down Grade's neck, the skin red and tender under his mouth.

"Say it," he rasped as he worked Grade's hole wider.

Grade squirmed in place, his breath quick and ragged as he tried to catch it. "Make me."

Clay chuckled against the crook of Grade's shoulder and then bit down roughly on the slope of muscle.

"I will," he said. "Like you said, you don't have all night. I fucking do."

Clay slid his hand over Grade's hip and across his tight, flat stomach. He could feel the twitch of muscle and skin under his palm as he lingered for a moment. Then he trailed his fingers down, through the sparse fluff of hair that arrowed down from Grade's navel, until he wrapped them roughly around Grade's cock. He twisted his hand as he pulled back, the thin skin creased under his grip.

"Fuck," Grade moaned and let his head fall back, his eyes squinted shut.

"Not until you say it," Clay said. He slid sticky fingers out of Grade's ass and wiped them on his leg. "What's the magic word?"

Rather than say it, Grade bit his lips together like a kid. Clay snorted, grabbed the back of Grade's head, and chewed his mouth open for a kiss. It was hard and impatient, all tongue and teeth and Grade's breath in Clay's mouth.

Clay pressed against Grade's back, his cock nudged up against the slippery crack of his ass, and—*fuck*—he wanted Grade to fold. He was so hard it hurt, the throb of his cock something he could feel in his spine. Except he'd run his mouth, and he didn't like to lose.

"Say please," he demanded around Grade's tongue in his mouth.

Grade tilted his head back, and maybe he was going to say it. If he was, it got lost in the groan that escaped him as Clay squeezed the base of his cock. His thumb pressed down, and he could feel the pulse of Grade's heartbeat as the blood was trapped.

"What was that?" he asked.

"Fuck you," Grade said. It would have had more bite if he'd not thrust his hips forward, fucking his cock into Clay's fist. "Please."

"Please what?" Clay asked.

"Fuck me," Grade begged as he gave in. "Clay. Please?"

Finally. Clay didn't know how long he could have dragged this out. He wasn't exactly known for his self-control when it came to what he wanted. And right now, he wanted Grade.

Clay let go of Grade's cock, ignoring the whimper of protest, and reached down between their bodies. The familiar touch—sex was always better with someone else, but nobody knew his cock like his own hand—zapped little jolts of sticky-sweet pleasure back into his balls. He rubbed his thumb along the shaft, up to the lip of the slick, flushed head, and pressed it against Grade's ass.

It slid between the lube-wet curves of taut muscle and stalled as it hit the wet, puckered hole. Clay bit the inside of his cheek as he felt the pressure ache down the length of his cock and into his balls. He flexed his fingers against Grade's shoulder, his weight braced on it, and pushed harder.

A raw, hungry noise escaped Grade's throat, and his splayed fingers dug into the wall as Clay's cock slid into him. He tipped his head forward to rest against his forearm, the exposed nape of his neck bare and vulnerable.

"I told you it was worth asking nice for," Clay said harshly, the words dry in his throat as his cock spread Grade's ass open around it. "You should have listened."

Grade snorted without lifting his head.

"If the sex wasn't good," he said, "I'd not be here."

"Far be it from me not to live up to expectations."

Clay buried himself in Grade with one last thrust, his crotch pressed against the curve of Grade's ass and the front of his dry-clean-only dress trousers wet with a mixture of pre-come and lube. He stayed there for a second, the clutch of Grade's ass warm and tight around him, while Grade swore softly into the wall.

The second he relaxed, the muscles across his back loosened into it, Clay hooked his arm around Grade's throat, fingers wrapped around the point of his shoulder, and fucked him.

Thoroughly.

Each stroke buried his cock deep inside Grade, his ass stretched wide around Clay's shaft, and Grade pushed back to meet him every time. The long muscles in his legs, taut and strained from the angle, trembled visibly under the skin as sweat dripped down his back. Clay brushed a kiss over Grade's shoulders, the faint spray of freckles where the sun got through the collar of his T-shirt traced with Clay's tongue. He could taste salt and a chemically sour smoke that stung the back of his throat.

The driving beat of the music rattled around in the back of his head and set the pace, quick and hard enough to jar a gasp out of Grade. He had to keep both arms braced, the wiry bands of muscle outlined through his pale skin, to keep from being fucked into the wall.

Since he couldn't take care of it for himself, Clay slid his free hand around to caress Grade's chest. He pinched the bud of a nipple and then soothed the small discomfort with a swipe of a callused thumb.

"God," Grade moaned. The word was drawn out over his tongue as he clenched his hands into fists, his knuckles pressed into the paintwork. "*Please.*"

Pleasure banked—sticky and hot as melted sugar—in his balls. They had a sort of dull heaviness that made him want to squirm and spilled out into the clenched muscles of his thighs and filled his spine up like pressure.

Each stroke spread Grade wider, slid just that *fraction* deeper. He moaned something fast and breathless—directions, it sounded like—as sweat dripped down his face and made his back wet. Clay ran his hand down Grade's stomach and back to his cock. He wrapped his hand around it and pumped his fist in rough time to the thrusts that jolted Grade's body.

Grade had asked nicely, after all. That meant he got to come first.

Which was going to be soon. Grade had lost his words, even the curses. All that was left were breathy, hungry whimpers. His body was pulled tight as a tripwire with it, ready to go off if you just… hit… it… right. Clay drove his cock into Grade harder, each thrust almost painful as it made his balls feel scalded because they were so heavy and tender. He could feel the release as it built up under Grade's skin—flutters in his muscles and the tension in clenched joints.

So close.

Clay kissed the nape of Grade's neck, right where his spine fed into his skull, and wrung his release out of him on hard strokes and callused fingers. It spilled sticky out of Grade and all over Clay's fingers. Drops of come splattered on the wall as well.

Pleasure left Grade boneless, sprawled against the wall. Clay fucked him like that for a second, limp dick still handled roughly as Grade moaned. Then he pulled him back off the wall so he was plastered against Clay's body, with Clay's cock still thick and hard inside him.

Two steps back put the arm of the couch against Clay's thighs. He dragged Grade with him and sat down, long legs folded over his. His hands on Grade's hips—what there was of those—meant he set the pace even once Grade found the presence of mind to brace his feet on the floor. His thighs were rock hard, clenched into knots, as he thrust himself down onto Clay's cock.

It didn't take long. Clay had hung on to his control with fishing line and the skin of his teeth. Now all it took was the squeeze of Grade's ass around his cock—and the hand he reached back to wrap around Clay's neck—to get him off

He thrust up hard into Grade and came inside him, a wet spill that he felt around his cock as it softened. They stayed there for a minute, Grade slumped back against Clay's chest and his cock glued to his thigh.

Until it made Clay's skin start to shrink-wrap itself over his bones. He rolled Grade off him and onto the couch, sprawled out lewdly on the leather.

"I need a smoke," he said as he stood up. His trousers were stained, and come smeared over his shirt, dried stiff and tacky on the loose tail. He tucked his cock away and zipped up. "Was this it? Or did you need something other than stress relief from me?"

Grade folded one arm back behind his head and scratched the inside of his thigh with the other.

"No," he said placidly. "That was it."

Clay grabbed his cigarettes and walked out into the kitchen. He propped the door open and leaned against the doorframe as he lit a cigarette.

That was probably it, he thought idly as he breathed smoke into the murky predawn light. The difference between a fuck buddy and a boyfriend—one of them would hang around even if the sex wasn't good.

Clay waited to feel something about that, but... fuck it. Like Clay was in this for the conversation, not the cock. Sometimes he had his own stress to work out.

He took another draw on his cigarette and exhaled slowly, his head tipped back and eyes closed.

"I thought you gave that up?" Grade commented as he joined Clay on the doorstep. He smelled of sex and Clay, and the sweatpants he'd pulled on didn't cover up much.

There was a hint of bleach too. Still.

"Yeah," Clay said. He offered the cigarette to Grade and was turned down with a shake of his head. Clay took another hit and then flicked the butt into the dark. The red-ember end spun for a second before disappearing in the long grass. "Then I started again."

He turned around to look at Grade. Clay reached out to cup one hand around the nape of Grade's neck, his thumb under Grade's chin.

"How confident are you that your staged crime scenes will completely fool the cops?" he asked.

Since he could—now—Clay started to unbutton his shirt. The tiny mother-of-pearl buttons were clumsy to manage with wet fingers. Once he had them all flicked loose, he pulled the shirt down over his shoulders and let it dangle by the collar from one hooked finger.

Grade stared at him, the confusion obvious on his face. "A bit late to ask now," he said.

"Indulge me," Clay said.

Grade hesitated a second longer and then gave up with a shrug. He rubbed his thumb along the sharp line of his jaw as he thought about it. Finally he grimaced and shook his head.

"It's not that simple. In LA—"

Clay rolled his eyes. It was out of habit. Grade gave him an annoyed look and pressed on.

"*In LA*, I knew the players involved and how they were likely to jump. It's not as easy here. We need everyone with a say in the case to take our staged version of events at face value," he said, then counted off the involved parties on his fingers. "The deputies, the coroner's office, and the family. I've given them an obvious cause of death and a crime that isn't that interesting, so hopefully, they'll buy it. Until they do, though, we're in limbo. All it takes is one person to start digging their heels in to throw up enough noise that the case gets more attention."

Clay went "huh" and headed back into the main room. His glass was dry, but the one he'd poured for Grade was still set out. He picked it up and took a swig, the bourbon sticky-sweet as it lingered on his tongue.

"Fisher didn't ask us to help Parker," Clay said. He didn't bother to look around. Instead, he swirled the glass in his hand and watched the bourbon spin. "Not any of his men either. Far as I know, they're in the dark about this. Ezra took a punt on offering a helping hand on his own. Figured it couldn't hurt to have a judge in his pocket."

It was possible that Grade wasn't as smart as he liked to believe he was, but he was smart enough to map out the various ways that could fuck up in their faces.

"He's going to get you killed one day," Grade said after a grim second.

Clay shrugged.

"Yeah, I know. I'm OK with that, though. It's the job, and not like I ever figured I'd die in bed surrounded by loved ones. Prison guards, maybe." Besides, if it weren't for Ezra, then Clay would have died, either in the desert with his skin melted into the sand or when he'd got back and discovered how few opportunities there were for a man with his unique combination of skills and PTSD. Clay tilted his head back to pour the last drops of bourbon into his mouth, then turned to look at Grade. "That's not what you signed up for, though. So consider this a heads-up in case things go south."

That was definitely too close to something real. The awkward hung in the air, thick enough to taste, until Grade cleared his throat uncomfortably.

"I... Clay, I appreciate you—"

"Yeah," Clay interrupted him. "If there is an afterlife, I don't want to listen to you whine for the rest of eternity about being buried in Kentucky. So try and avoid it. I'm going to bed. You can let yourself out."

He slung his shirt over his shoulder and headed upstairs. The pressure in the back of his brain—the compulsion to fuck up somehow—had vented enough that he could probably sleep. If he couldn't, there was another bottle of bourbon he could crack open.

Clay stripped his trousers off as he stepped into his bedroom and left them in a ball on the floor. He could have probably done with a shower, but he didn't feel like washing the smell of sex off his skin just yet. So he just sprawled out on the bed, pillows stuffed behind his head, and idly picked at the matted hair on his stomach as he waited.

It took a minute before Grade came into the room and crawled onto the bed with him. The tension in Clay's shoulders relaxed enough that he had to admit how tight they'd been. It would have meant something if Grade had left. It was hard to say what exactly—not like either of them had ever talked about this—but it was hardly going to be anything good.

Clay folded one arm behind his head and raised his eyebrows at Grade.

"I thought you didn't have all night?" he said.

Grade propped himself up on his elbow. "You want me to go?"

Clay reached up to scruff the back of Grade's neck and pull him down, sprawled over Clay's chest.

"Shut up," he told him.

DIRTY JOB

CHAPTER SEVEN

"LAUNDRY OR SCHOOL run?"

Grade stopped at the back door. The kitchen smelled like his childhood: cleaning supplies, oatmeal scorched to the bottom of the metal pot, and a certain amount of panic. He rubbed the back of his neck and watched Dory and his mom dodge around each other and the table in the small space.

"We have microwave oatmeal," he said.

Dory bumped the freezer door shut with her hip and waved her hand at their mom. "I told her that," she said. "But would she listen? Well, maybe now her *favorite* child has spoken, she'll finally listen to me."

Oh.

Oh no.

Grade grimaced to himself and leaned back against the doorframe, sort of out of the line of fire. He should have kept his mouth shut. That would have been the smart move. Harry had finally texted him that the Lexus was sorted, which was one thing less to worry about. Instead of getting to enjoy that, now he was in the middle of the Annual Mother/Daughter Pulaski Throwdown.

Their mom grabbed the scorched pot off the stove and dropped it into the sink. The metal sizzled as it hit the water. She added dish soap and flicked the tap on to fill the pot as she turned to glare at Dory, her hand on her hip. Susie Pulaski was fifty-two years old. She'd been married to a petty criminal and raised two children on her own. She'd not gotten anywhere in life by admitting to the reality of her situation—whether that was to do with her cooking, her still definitely naturally red hair, or that neither of her children was going to make her a doctor's mother-in-law.

"Can you put a mother's love in the microwave?" she demanded. "Is that what we can do?"

"You can at least put microwave oatmeal in your stomach," Dory said as she threw her hands up. She was still dressed for work, in hot pants and boots, with an old sweater thrown on over the top for the drive home. "Which is more than can be said for that bit of black gravel you made. And that's nice, Mom. Real nice. Don't even try and deny he's your favorite."

Susie started to clear the table. Bowls rattled against each other as she stacked them up next to the sink.

"I don't need to dignify that with a denial," she said. "I love both of my children equally, and Cody's my favorite."

"Yeah, but I pushed him out of me," Dory said, "so I should get some credit for that. What's Grade ever given you? Except piles."

"Hold on," Grade said. "How did I get involved in this?"

Dory turned and gave him a scathing look. "You'd know," she said, "if you weren't a dirty stop-out. Are those even your clothes?"

They weren't. Grade glared at Dory anyhow, because she knew whose clothes they were, and that was *not* a conversation that Grade wanted to have with his mom. Not yet. Not ever.

"I was working," he said.

Dory narrowed her eyes, gold mascara patchy on her lashes, at him. "Doing what?"

"Uber Eats."

Frustration creased Dory's whole face, and she stamped her foot. "Oh my God," she said. "That is such a shit lie! You're a shit liar and a shit brother, yet here you are—God's gift."

She burst into tears and stormed out of the room. She slammed the kitchen door behind her and then, a second later, shoved it back open again.

"I'm not fucking sad!" she said. "I'm mad. So leave me the fuck alone."

Susie waved a finger at her. "Language!"

"I'm a fucking adult!"

"In my house."

Dory laughed and spread her arms. "Oh, and there we are," she said. "Your house. Thanks. Thanks for the reminder my life is just shit and I got nothing."

She slammed out of the room again.

Susie sniffed and pushed her sleeves up to her elbows. She grabbed a pot scrubber and shoved both hands into the hot water.

"Well?" she asked. "Do you want to do the school or the laundry run?"

"What was that about?" Grade asked.

Instead of an answer, Susie just started to scrub more aggressively at the pan, until she suddenly stopped. She pulled her hands out of the sink—bubbles flipped everywhere—and in a burst of frustration hauled the pot over to the trash bin, stamped on the lever to pop the lid, and threw the whole thing in.

"Mom?" Grade prodded. "What happened?"

"If you—" Susie stopped whatever she'd been going to say, which meant it had been mean. That was OK. Grade could probably fill that in from there for himself. She looked around for a dish towel, and when she couldn't find one, she dried her hands on the hem of her T-shirt. "I don't know. She's just in one of her moods. Again. Still. She'll get through it. We'll get through it."

She sniffed and wiped under her eyes with a still damp hand. Grade knew better than to comment on that.

"Anyhow," Susie said briskly. "What is it? Laundry run or school?"

"Laundry," Grade said after a second.

Susie nodded and rolled her sleeves back down. "Right," she said. "I'd better go and get Cody. He had a sleepover, so I said we'd pick both of them up this morning."

She got her coat on and Cody's lunch from the fridge. Then she grabbed her keys from the hook and paused as she looked Grade up and down. Her eyebrows rose at the jeans, which exposed a bit more ankle than usual.

"Is he nice?" she asked.

"No."

Susie sighed and shook her head. "I don't know where the two of you get your taste in men from," she tutted.

That made Grade do a double take. He stared at his mom. "You *don't*?" he said. "What, are you telling me we were adopted?"

She tched at him. "Tommy was a good man," she said.

"Bullshit."

Susie slapped his shoulder and pushed him out of the way. "He always treated me like gold," she said. "And he was a good father, don't forget that."

"He was a criminal," Grade pointed out.

"Said the pot to the kettle," Susie said as she opened the back door. She raised her eyebrows at him and then sniffed, "Uber Eats, my ass."

She closed the door behind her with a triumphant click before Grade had a chance to say anything. Grade spluttered at the closed door for a moment.

"And I'd not call myself a good person," he muttered at last.

The door didn't care. Grade scrubbed his hand over his face and rubbed his eyes, which were dry and tired despite the few hours he'd grabbed in Clay's bed. He could have got a few more, but the morning sex had been worth the trade-off.

He looked around the chaos in the kitchen for a moment. Then he put the kettle on the stove.

Grade rapped his knuckles against the door.

"Fuck off," Dory's muffled voice told him.

He let himself in.

Dory was facedown on the bed, her booted feet awkwardly dangling off the edge. When she heard the door creak, she lifted her head enough to glare at him.

"I told you to fuck off," she said. "How much clearer do I have to be that I don't want to talk to you?"

"I mean, you could have locked the door," Grade said. He sat on the floor next to the bed, legs folded under him, and held up the mug. "I made you some tea."

Nothing happened. The sides of the mug were hot enough to burn Grade's fingers as he waited. Then Dory took it.

"You still suck," she said.

"I do," Grade said. "Ask Clay."

"Arrggh!" Dory spluttered. The bed bounced against Grade's shoulders as she rolled away from him and—he checked over his shoulder—sat up. "That's disgusting. I don't want to think about that. Weirdo."

She sat back against her pillows, knees pulled up, and sulkily drank her tea.

Grade looked around the room. He'd been in here since he got back, but it never ceased to catch him off guard.

"It's always strange to come in here," he said. "My room is just the same as it was when I left. Same posters. Same books. You have framed photos and everything."

"That's because I never left," Dory said. "It's not like your apartment in LA had K-Pop posters on the wall, did it?"

That wasn't a question that Grade wanted to answer. In his defense, the posters had covered some disturbing holes and stains. He waited for a moment and then changed the subject.

"Is all this because of what happened? With Buchanan?" he asked.

"When I was kidnapped, tied up, threatened, and nearly got killed? No!" Dory said sharply. Then she looked down into the cup and, in a softer voice, corrected herself. Her mousy brown roots were showing up under the light pink. "I mean, it should be, but it isn't. Not really."

"So it's not my fault?" Grade asked.

Dory looked up and gave him an aggrieved look. "Not everything is about you, Grade."

He hooked his arm onto the bed and pulled himself up. "In that case," he said, "why are you being such a cow to me?"

Dory didn't look up as she shrugged, her hands wrapped tightly around the mug.

"Just felt shitty," she said. "I wanted to share."

"Work?" Grade asked. "Has someone been bothering you?"

"No more than usual," Dory said. She looked up and pulled a face at whatever Grade's expression looked like. "Oh, don't look at me like that. Work is nothing I can't handle, nothing I didn't handle when you weren't here. You don't have to sic your boyfriend on anyone."

"Well, you didn't have to sic Mom on me," Grade said. "But you did anyhow."

Dory handed him the mug and leaned over the side of the bed to grab the strap of her backpack. She hefted it up off the floor and into her lap so she could search through it. While he waited for her to finish, Grade took a sip of tea. He nearly spat it back into the cup. He'd forgotten how many sugars Dory took, even though he'd been the one to spoon them in.

"There's this guy that comes to the Choke. Verne," she said. "He's usually one of Alina's regulars, but a couple of weeks ago she got Covid, and I covered her shift. Verne likes to talk."

"You should get extra for that," Grade said.

Dory gave him an aggrieved look through her lashes. "Not like that," she said. "Just conversation."

"I know," Grade said. "That's my point."

"This thing you have with Traynor?" Dory said as she pulled an envelope out of the bag and handed it to him. "You need to lock that down because I don't know who else would want you."

There was money in the envelope. Grade had a lot of experience with discreet packets of cash, and he'd say there was about a couple of grand here. It was thinner than most people expected. He turned the envelope over. The flap at the back had been peeled up and stuck back down, bits of it torn and wrinkled.

"Are you paying me to go away?" he asked. "That will work."

Dory made an annoyed sound as she took the cup of tea off him. "Verne's a skip tracer," she said. "A good one, apparently. I told him about Dad and asked if he had any tips, and he offered to look into it for us."

The "us" made Grade bite his tongue before he said something he'd regret. He'd never bought into Dory's faith that Dad would come back one day. Tommy Pulaski was either dead and *couldn't* come back, or he'd dumped his family for 100 grand in stolen drugs and just *wouldn't*.

But Grade's penance for getting Dory dragged into the Buchanan mess was that he didn't get to argue with her about it anymore. That was harder for him than it should be. Luckily there were plenty of other things to argue about.

"Dory, people will say a lot of shit for two grand."

"I wave my titties around for tips," Dory said. "I know what people will do for money. Better than you."

"Sure," Grade said. "Because I don't do anything gross for cash."

Dory gave him a thin, smug slice of a smile. "Don't talk about Traynor that way, Grade." She ignored the face Grade pulled at her. "It's not like I just took his word for it. I checked him and ran down his references. He's legit. Lonely, but legit."

Shit. It would have been easier for Grade if she'd not done that. As it was, she'd done her research, thought about the pitfalls, and...

"It's your money," Grade said reluctantly as he handed the money back. "I don't think it's a good idea, but it's not my call. You can do what you want."

"Wow," Dory deadpanned. "Can I really?"

She didn't take the envelope, though. Grade put it down on the bedspread between them and waited.

"Besides, you're a bit late," Dory said finally. She finished her tea and leaned over to set the mug on the nightstand. "I already gave him the money. A couple of months ago after—after what happened."

That meant, Grade supposed, that it sort of was his fault after all.

"And what?" he asked. "Now he needs some more money to pay a bribe or hire a hacker? Come on, Dory. You know better than that. He salted you."

"I'm not an idiot," Dory said. "And he gave the money back. He said he couldn't find anything—not even a dead end—and he wasn't in the habit of charging for failure. So fuck you. Turns out there's still at least one good guy out there, if you'd like his number."

"That's not really my demographic," Grade said. "And he just took his expenses?"

Dory shook her head and finally lifted the envelope. She picked at the flap with a bitten-short thumbnail, a rim of chewed-off blue polish down around the quick.

"No, this is all of it," she said and pulled a face. "I guess I just looked that pathetic: a stripper with daddy issues. How cliche is that?"

Grade reached out and took her hand. "Doreen Pulaski—"

She made an aggrieved noise and tried to pull her hand away from him. "Don't call me that."

"You are a neurotic train wreck of a human being," he said. "The 'daddy issues' are just the tip of your neurotic iceberg."

"I'm not sure that should make me feel better," Dory said.

"But it does," Grade said.

Dory rolled her eyes, but she didn't disagree with him. After a second, she moved her hand away and pulled her knees up, her arms wrapped around them and the quilt wrinkled under her boots. She rested her chin on the bony ledge she'd made, flicked a picked-off bit of envelope flap onto the bed, and sighed.

"Did I upset Mom?"

"Oh, thanks," Grade said. "I'm glad you're worried about my feelings."

"Like you'd admit it if I did," Dory said as she glanced up at him through her lashes.

That was fair enough, Grade supposed.

"Mom's OK," he said. "She agreed with you that Uber Eats was a bad lie."

Dory pulled a "duh" face at him. "You know we don't even *have* Uber Eats round here, right?" she asked.

Grade shrugged. "I honestly didn't think even Sweeny was that shit," he said. "I just don't get why you're this upset, Dory. It was a swing and a miss on finding Dad, but not for the first time."

There was silence for a second as Dory struggled for an answer. Finally, she just shook her head, faded pink hair falling forward to hide her face.

"Esme Rawlins," she said and looked up at Grade expectantly.

That name was… not… familiar. Grade racked his brain and then had to give up with an apologetic shrug.

"My best friend," Dory said. "The only one who stuck around after—well, after Cody. She's getting married."

Grade ducked his head to catch Dory's eye. "She didn't invite you?"

Dory sighed. "Oh, worse than that," she said. "She wants me to be her maid of honor, and I'm such a miserable bitch I can't even be happy for her. I hope she gets stung by hornets and her head is bigger than her tits on the day."

"What is it?" Grade asked. "The husband or the dad walking her down the aisle?"

Dory made an annoyed noise at him and got up off the bed. She brushed herself off and then gestured down her body.

"Look at me," she said. "You think if I wanted a husband, I couldn't get one? Of course it's the fucking dad thing."

She stalked over to the side table and grabbed a handful of wipes to clean her face. If she scrubbed extra hard around her eyes... well, eye makeup could be hard to get off. The last time Grade had twinked it up, it had taken three days before he stopped getting bits of glitter in his eyes.

"I want my dad," she said eventually. "If I ever get married—"

"You will," Grade reassured her.

She gave him an annoyed look in the mirror. "What? I don't get a choice? Maybe I don't want to get married, Grade."

"Seriously?" Grade spluttered indignantly.

"If," Dory said again, emphasizing the word. "If I get married *or* go to college *or* become a mechanic, he's not going to be there. It'll be Mom, who'll say something about how I could have done this earlier if I'd not gotten pregnant."

"I'll be there," Grade said.

The last bit of glossy highlighter smeared away under the oily wipe. Dory blew her nose into the makeup-smeared tissue and then crumpled it up to throw in the trash bin. Then she met his gaze in the mirror.

"No," she said, "you won't. Just like you weren't here for anything else. And that's fine. I get it. You *know* I get it. Just don't lie about it."

Grade broke the reflected eye contact first. It wasn't fair, but she wasn't wrong either. Sometimes things were like that. People didn't always get what they deserved, good or bad. Grade couldn't change who he was, and he couldn't bring their dad back.

They'd all just have to live with that.

He got up off the bed and poked at a knotted tangle of jeans and swimsuit on the floor with the toe of his sneaker.

"Are these for the laundry?" he asked.

Dory turned to look at him, a pot of cream held in one hand. "You're doing the laundry?"

"If I'd picked the school run, Cody would be running pretty late."

"OK," Dory said, drawing the word out over her tongue. She patted the air like she had to soothe it. "It's OK. We can deal with this. There's no need to worry."

"I'm not."

"You should be," Dory said. "You ruin one of my work outfits and I'll gut you."

"I can do laundry," Grade said. "Or did you think I just bought new clothes every day in LA?"

"The way you dress, who cares," Dory said as she wiped the excess cream onto her elbows. "I'm not spending the next six months wondering if I've put on weight or if you've shrunk my jeans. You go and pick up anything lying on the floor of Cody's room, and I'll get my stuff ready and meet you downstairs."

She made shooing gestures at him with both hands and looked expectant. Grade glared at her.

"You know this is part of what I do for a living?" he said.

"And if I needed to get blood out of my Miu Miu rip-off skirt, that'd be great," Dory said. "But I need you to pre-treat the baby oil stains on my sequined booty shorts. So just do what you're told."

• 94 •

"You remember that you're the little sister, yeah?" Grade asked.

"I'll drive."

"And I always enjoy your company," Grade said. "I'll see you downstairs in fifteen minutes."

§

The laundromat hadn't changed.

Same nicotine-colored machines, same cut and greasy linoleum on the floor, and the same caked slots you had to slam with the heel of your hand to get the money to drop in. Even the clientele was the same. Grade nodded to Mrs. Fowler, who'd taught them both history, and got the expected look of suspicion in return. The woman, her artificially baby blond hair still in the bob he remembered, grabbed her bag, clutched it tightly, and stomped down to the other end of the room to mutter aggrievedly to a middle-aged woman placidly pairing socks.

"I still got it," he said to Dory.

"She hates Cody too," Dory said. She'd changed into jeans and stolen one of Cody's sweaters, her hair scraped back in a skimpy ponytail. Before Grade could just stuff everything into the drum of the machine, she pulled out a handful of mesh bags and handed half of them to Grade. "Sequins in one. Lace in the other."

"They're all clothes."

"Just sort."

Grade sighed, but he got pissy when people tried to tell him how to do his job. He started to sort them out quickly—interrupted by the occasional "that's not silk, it's rayon" protest from Dory—so they could get on with this. Once he accepted it was going to be done, he found it quite relaxing.

Precise, repetitive work always was. It turned his brain down a notch.

Halfway through, the steady background chatter of a quiz show cut out and was replaced by the blare of an advertisement and then a smooth, practiced voice. Grade glanced up and caught the tail end of some school event on the news.

Mrs. Fowler waved the remote at the screen, her finger jabbed down on the volume button as she tried to turn it up.

"I saw the first report this morning before I left the house," she said in an aside to her friend. "They didn't have many details then."

Her friend tched her tongue against her teeth. "It's terrible. And such a nice neighborhood."

The house on the TV looked different in daylight, fenced off behind strips of yellow police tape. Behind the reporter, police roamed in and out of the house, bags of what shouldn't be evidence if Grade had done his job right in their hands.

"...behind me, the police are still in Ms. Ledger's house," the round-faced woman said as she squinted into the wind. She hooked her hair out of her face with one hand as she went on. "Sheriff Anderson has yet to confirm whether this could be related to Ms. Ledger's work at the Cargill County District Attorney's office."

Shit.

"I'm telling you," Fowler said, voice pitched to carry and nearly drowning out the reporter. "It's not just Sweeny. Doglan has gone to hell too, just criminals and whores everywhere you look."

Next to him, Dory had stopped mid-sort, a camisole dangling from her fingers as she watched the news play out.

"Although Ledger, then an assistant district attorney," the reporter went on, "was not directly involved in the 2019 investigation into the use of jailhouse informants, she was still forced to resign in the wake of the scandal."

It was his own fault, Grade thought grimly. He'd had a bad feeling about this job from the start; he should have listened to his instincts. It didn't matter how Clay had spun subcontracting, it was still working for an amateur.

"Poor woman," Dory said. "I hope they catch whoever killed her."

That was family loyalty for you.

DIRTY JOB

CHAPTER EIGHT

CLAY PULLED UP outside the one and only Catholic church in Sweeny, a small stone building that was currently tucked in between a charity shop and a rundown Subway.

The Baptists had gotten all the good real estate around here.

He parked the bike up on the curb and pulled his helmet off to hang it on the handlebars. One of the old women on their way out, propped up on each other's arm as they headed down the street, gave him a disapproving look.

"You missed mass again, Clay," Deirdre Mills said and tched her tongue against her teeth. "How am I ever going to introduce you to my granddaughter if you don't make a respectable man of yourself?"

Clay used his heel to put the kickstand down and tilted the bike over onto it. He swung his leg off it and gave the old lady his best charming-bastard grin. Old ladies loved a bad boy.

"I thought that was what a good woman was for, Ms. Danvers," he said. "To make a man respectable."

The other old woman, Ellie Benson, gave Clay a scathing look over the top of her glasses.

"It's 2022, Mr. Traynor," she said tartly. "Young women today have better things to do than rehabilitate assholes."

"And God doesn't?"

"Don't blaspheme," Deirdre said.

At the same time, Ellie lifted a finger heavenwards. "He," she said, "signed up for the job."

Clay shoved his keys into the pocket of his jacket.

"Next time," he promised with a wink that made Deirdre cackle. Ellie tutted at her friend for being easily pleased while Clay headed into the church. It smelled like floor polish, candles, and stewed cabbage from the weekend soup kitchen.

Habit made Clay dip his fingers in the font on the way in. He dampened his brow and balls on autopilot, the flick of his fingers to each shoulder an old habit pinched into Clay by his grandmother.

The soft murmur of prayers, cut through with the familiar murmur of the rosary being said, provided a muted background sound as Clay paused in the doorway to look around. His gaze flicked over a couple of nuns sat in the middle, heads bowed over their rosaries, and a couple of homeless men sitting quietly in the back as they drank from thin plastic cups of soup.

A couple of them were probably ex-military. Father Gilmore had talked to Clay before about some sort of outreach to the local homeless vets, to give them some idea what services were available to them. Clay had dodged it every time so far.

What the fuck was he going to say? Clay hadn't exactly come back Stateside and made civilian society his bitch. He'd no idea how some people made it work for them, how they went from mortars and machine gun fire to 2.4 kids and a nine-to-five job.

That particular weird mix of imposter syndrome and guilt wasn't what Clay was here for, though. He gave a stiff nod of acknowledgment to one of the men who'd looked over—got the same back—and headed down the aisle to the front of the church.

He pulled a fifty out of his pocket for the collection box and picked up one of the little battery-operated candles to turn it on.

It didn't have quite the same feeling of ritual as a real candle, waxy against his hand, and the smoky sizzle of a freshly lit match, but that was a fire hazard, and these were cheaper.

Clay set the little light back in its holder. It flickered dimly. He didn't know why he bothered. If he'd still believed in God, he'd not have done half the things he'd done. And nobody he knew who did would want Clay's prayers. It just felt right. Like he'd let something go.

And if anyone was here to meet him, they could come and find him.

It took a minute, but finally someone stepped up next to Clay. The man was narrow and a bit shorter than Clay, in a button-down shirt and slacks. Clay didn't know him, but something about him did look vaguely familiar. The man cleared his throat as he reached for one of the lights.

"Mr. Adams?" he asked.

"He couldn't make it," Clay said. "I'm his associate."

The man fumbled with the plastic disc and nearly dropped it. He grabbed it with both hands and gave Clay a quick, suspicious look.

"How do I know that's true?" he asked.

Clay sighed. "What the fuck do you think I'm going to do?" he asked. "Produce a letter of introduction? If I was lying, I'd have just told you I was Ezra. You've obviously got no fucking clue what he looks like."

The man turned the candle over twice, as if he had never seen one before. He finally thumbed the switch on and set it back down to flicker.

"I was told to speak to Mr. Adams, no one else," the man said. "He told our mutual friend that he'd meet me here."

"His kid bit someone at daycare," Clay said, "so he asked me to step in. I'd apologize, but if you're here, then it looks like Judge Parker couldn't make it either."

The man clenched his jaw, muscles visible in knots under his skin, and glanced around quickly. There was no one close enough to overhear. Despite that, the man gave Clay a hard look.

"Keep her name out of your mouth," he said stiffly. "And my employer can't be seen to be associated with... dubious sorts... especially in the middle of an election. They need to keep as much deniability as possible. Can we go somewhere more private?"

Clay turned to look the man up and down. Then he pursed his lips and raised his eyebrows.

"You want to fuck?" he asked.

The man looked coldly angry for a moment. "You?" he said. "No."

Clay grinned, slow and lazy, as he decided if he was pissed off or not. It wasn't like he'd wanted Parker's errand boy to jump on the offer, but still. Errand Boy had enough wit to look uncomfortable as Clay stared at him for a long, slow second.

"Then if you want, we can stay here," Clay said. He tipped his head toward the empty front pew. "Or you can fuck off."

He walked over to the pew and sat down, one arm slung over the wooden back of it. The nun's disapproval across the aisle was palpable. After a moment, Errand Boy came over too. He sat stiffly upright, far enough away that the frayed cuff of Clay's jacket didn't touch him.

"What does Parker want?" he asked.

"I told you—" Errand Boy snapped.

Clay shifted slightly and dropped his hand on Errand Boy's shoulder. He tightened his grip until the man squirmed, his mouth gone white at the corners.

"The only thing you tell me is what I ask you about," Clay said. "Or I'll break your collarbone."

Errand Boy's nostrils flared. "You wouldn't dare," he said. "There's witnesses."

"There are," Clay agreed. "Nuns and all. After I break your collarbone, they'll all run over to ask what happened. Then, like a good little boy, you'll tell them what?"

"That you—" Errand Boy stopped as he heard his voice rise. He pressed his lips together and forced it back down to a hiss. "I'll tell them you're a pervert that hit on me and attacked me when I said no."

Clay nodded. "And they'll call the cops," Clay said. "Even before we get to the little favor I did your boss, is that whole scenario the sort of thing she wants to associate herself with?"

He waited. Errand Boy glared at him for a moment, then grimaced and nodded. "OK," he said through tight lips. "I get it."

Clay let go.

Errand Boy scooted away down the bench. As if he thought Clay wouldn't get up to kick his ass. It was fine, though; his cologne was a bit sickly to start with.

"My employer," Errand Boy said as he stared up at the crucifix with fixed attention, "wants to know if the robbery two nights ago had anything to do with you."

"There were a few," Clay said. "But the one related to our business with your boss? Yeah, that was us."

"This morning," Errand Boy said, "Mr. Collymore's body was found on the mountain. Apparently the police think he's been there since the night of the party."

He pushed himself to his feet. Errand Boy grabbed his sleeve and then thought better of it. He let go and stood up too, body angled as if they were just having a conversation.

"Your associate needs to tell my employer who was involved," he said. "The police reports say that there were three men that night, and we want to know who they are and who they work for."

"Anything else?" Clay asked.

It was meant to be sarcastic, but apparently Errand Boy thought it was a chance to tag one more thing onto the list.

"An accounting of what happened to Ms. Ledger's belongings," Errand Boy said. "You weren't hired to line your pockets by stealing those things from the house, and our mutual benefactor doesn't want to get caught because whatever inbred you hired to pull this off gets arrested selling a nice necklace in a shitty part of town. The expectation is that you make this right."

"Or?" Clay asked, intrigued about the answer.

Errand Boy faltered. "Or… or she'll have to involve other people. That's not what she wants to do. But she will."

"I'll pass that on," Clay said. "And you pass this on too. We did exactly what we were asked to do, and if your boss has buyer's remorse now, that's her problem. If she wants to keep her hands clean, tell her to keep them out of our business."

Errand Boy's eye twitched again. He reached up to rub at it and then dropped his hand self-consciously when he realized Clay had noticed.

"You think she wants them there?" he asked. "All my employer has ever done is try and protect the people she represents, the ideals that she stood up for. Now one stupid, horrible mistake could ruin all that? No. That's not fair. And it's not fair that Ms. Ledger's family lose more than they already have. We want everything that was taken back, and before this goes any further, we need to know who else knows about this."

Clay shrugged. "Like I said, I'll pass it on." He nodded toward the candles. "And remember to leave a donation for the Church. God only takes cash, not credit."

He walked out. One of the homeless men—Clay thought it was the one he'd nodded to—had lingered by the door. He had a tattoo on his forearm, just visible under his rolled-back sleeve, and held himself like he'd had a drill instructor spit in his face before.

"Everything OK?" the man asked. He nodded toward Errand Boy and then looked back at Clay. "You in trouble with whoever he works for?"

Clay turned to look at Errand Boy and then shrugged as he turned back to the stranger.

"If I'm not today, I will be tomorrow," he said. "Don't worry about it, but thanks."

He traded nods with the man and headed out of the church to get back on his bike.

§

Ezra popped the cap off the beer bottle against the edge of the table. Foam spilled out over his knuckles. He flicked it into the bushes on the side of the patio and then licked the rest of the damp off his fingers.

"What the fuck is she trying to pull?" he asked quietly.

Clay shrugged. He pulled a chair out with one boot and turned it around so he could sit in it backwards, his arms folded across the low back. There was a pool, chalky blue and serene, to the side of him. He could smell the chlorine from where he sat. The shell of a party—balloons, empty trestle tables stacked with tableware and folded tablecloths, a box of fireworks—was already set up around it.

"Like Grade said, never work with amateurs."

Ezra paced instead of sitting down. He took a swig of the beer and then used the bottle to gesture.

"Charity Parker has been in Fisher's pocket since she started out as a public defender," he said. "This isn't her first rodeo."

"First time she's gotten her hands dirty, though," Clay pointed out. He took a drink from his own beer and rested it against his thigh, the base of it leaving a smudged damp ring on his jeans. "She's used to being the one calling the shots, and now—when her life is on the line—she's stuck hoping that we know what we're doing. Could be she's just a backseat driver."

"Maybe," Ezra said. "We can hope."

He scratched at his arm absently, the scar from TJ still raised and red from Clay's hatchet patch-up drop. "You might as well say it."

Clay took a leisurely drink. "Say what?"

"That you told me so."

"I'm saving that for when we know I was right," Clay said. He leaned over to set the bottle down on the table and tilted his chin in the direction of the house behind Ezra. Three men headed their way. "Heads up. Incoming."

Ezra grimaced sourly, then schooled his face into a neutral expression as he turned around to watch Fisher come down the short flight of stairs to the patio. The apex predator of Kentucky crime had flour on his hands and a Kiss the Cook apron on. The gun in a shoulder holster under his arm was on brand, though.

"Mr. Adams," Fisher said crisply. He turned to look at Clay, and his voice turned silky. "And Clay."

That wasn't how this sort of thing usually went. Clay raised his eyebrows at Ezra, who looked suspicious but gave Clay the nod to take point.

"S'up?" Clay said dryly as he picked up the beer to toss off a toast.

Fisher smiled thinly and wiped his hands on his apron as he walked over to the table and took a seat. His two associates took up position behind him. One of them Clay didn't know, but he'd crossed paths with the other before.

"Nesmith," he said. "Come down in the world?"

The last time he'd seen Nesmith the well-dressed crook had been Fisher's second-in-command, not the hired muscle. The question made Nesmith smile thinly as he adjusted the fall of his jacket.

"You better hope not," he said. "Since I'm the one who vouched for you two after the Buchanan incident."

Fisher half turned in his seat and snapped his fingers at the other man to get his attention. "Get me a beer," he said. "Hal?"

Nesmith glanced at his watch and shrugged. "Sure," he said. "I've got to meet our lawyer at the court later, but one beer won't put me over the limit."

Clay didn't even bother to try and attach the "Hal" to his mental profile of Nesmith. It had taken him long enough to promote him from "Mouthpiece." He didn't care enough to try and do it again.

They waited in awkward silence as the other man got the beers and brought them over, already open. Fisher took a long draft on his, throat working as he swallowed, and wiped his mouth on the back of his hand.

"I'm baking a cake," he said. "It's thirsty work."

Clay picked up his beer and dangled it between his fingers. "I've got no idea what's going on here," he said. "Ezra?"

"I think we were both expecting a slightly more volatile conversation," Ezra said. "Based on your reputation, Mr. Fisher."

Fisher grinned and leaned back in his chair. "Because you think I'm a bad bastard?" Fisher asked. "I am, but everyone needs a little downtime. This is mine."

He picked flour from under his thumbnail.

"We had a CO who did this," Clay said. "Very approachable, very down to earth. He liked the things we liked."

"Sounds like a fun boss," Fisher said.

"He was an asshole," Clay said. "That's why he had to run so hard to try and stay ahead of it. So, for the record, unless you made that cake for me, I don't give a shit about it. Why are we here, Mr. Fisher?"

Fisher's expression didn't slip. He waited a moment, pulled his mouth down in a shrug, and looked at Ezra.

"Is that how you feel?" he asked.

"I'd have wrapped it up prettier," Ezra said. "But yeah. More or less. This was a meeting you asked for. I assume it wasn't to tell us about your hobby. What do you want?"

Fisher picked at a pasted-over bubble on the label of the beer with his thumbnail as he absorbed that. Then he relaxed and smirked as he took a drink.

"Your cleaner," he said. "The one that was involved in the Buchanan case. Pulaski."

The skin across Clay's shoulders tightened uncomfortably.

Ezra didn't look at him, but he didn't need to. They'd worked together long enough that Clay could feel the "stay fucking calm" vibes from his partner. Ezra sauntered over to the table and set his bottle down.

"Do you want a reference?" Ezra asked.

Fisher shook his head. "We handle disposal in-house," he said. "I don't trust freelancers."

"A date?" Clay asked. His head was full of static from *not* reacting, and he was mildly surprised at how calm his voice sounded.

Fisher's smile didn't slip. "Maybe for my wife's birthday, if he swings that way," he said. "No, I want to know what he's told you about Tommy Pulaski and where the bastard is holed up."

"Six feet under somewhere," Ezra said. "From what I've heard."

Fisher shook his head and looked at the bottle in his hand. "A lot of people think that," he said. "I know better."

"Sounds like you're the one with the inside track here," Clay said. "What do you need Grade for?"

He weighed the bottle in his hand, glass cold against his fingers, and let his mind run through the various scenarios that ended with him holding a gun. None of them ended with him walking out with a gun, or him walking out.

"Because my inside track is thirteen years old," Fisher said. "I know where Tommy Pulaski was then—and that he wasn't as dead as everyone thought—but what fucking good to me is that? I can't exactly carjack Doctor Who and time travel back there, can I? I need to know where I can find him now. Today."

"Why?" Ezra asked. "If he's alive, there's not going to be much of that hundred grand left. Not by now."

Fisher traded a look with Nesmith. The conversation was brief and silent—pursed lips, raised eyebrows, a final dip of the chin—and ended with Fisher standing up.

"Oh, the hundred grand isn't what I'm after," he said as he set the beer bottle down on the table. "Six months after he disappeared with the drugs, Tommy Pulaski killed my brother. That's what I want to have a word with him about. So either you find out where he is from his son or bring Pulaski Junior here so I can get it out of him. I'm easy. Either way. I'll give you a couple of weeks to decide which it's going to be. Now, if you'll excuse me, I have to get the cake out of the oven."

He walked away. The nameless muscle followed him; Nesmith stayed where he was and took a long, meditative drink of his beer.

"It's his stepson's birthday," Nesmith said finally. "There is actually a cake. He wants the boy to have a normal life, be a CPA or something."

Ezra finally looked at Clay. He shook his head slightly and then turned his attention back to Nesmith.

"That's good to know," Ezra said. "You know that Tommy Pulaski is dead, right?"

Nesmith shrugged. "What I know is that isn't what Mr. Fisher believes," he said. "And he thinks if Mr. Pulaski was alive six months after he disappeared… he could still be. That is what is important. At least it should be to you if you want to stay affiliated with our organization. Fisher would rather Tommy Pulaski not get any warning that his sabbatical is running out. That's why he wants you to deal with this instead. End of the day, though, that was his brother, and if he needs to take direct action, he will. Don't get in his way."

Ezra held up his hands, beer bottle still loosely gripped in one, to fend off that suggestion.

"I thought we'd made clear with Buchanan that crossing Fisher — in any way — is the last thing we want."

Nesmith raised his eyebrows and turned in his chair to face Clay. He pointed a finger across the table.

"What Buchanan made clear," he said, "is that Mr. Traynor here is a very capable man, and I'd hate to see him make a very bad decision over some white-trash ass. So consider this your one and only warning. That won't end well for you."

It was his turn to stand up and check his watch again. He drained his beer and set the dead bottle on the table.

"I have a meeting at court to get to," he said. "But feel free to stay and finish your beers. I'll send someone down who can show you out once you're finished. And for the record, I was impressed with how you handled the Buchanan situation. So was Fisher. Don't piss this opportunity up against a wall, gentlemen."

He walked away, headed back into the house after Fisher.

"So no cake for us?" Clay asked.

Ezra waited until Nesmith was out of earshot and then looked at Clay. "I don't suppose there's any way to talk you *out* of pissing this opportunity against the wall?" he asked.

"Let's be honest, Ez," Clay said as he finished his beer. "You're going to have a job on your hands talking me out of pissing in the pool on our way out."

Ezra set his bottle down on the table. "That's what I thought," he said. "OK. How about we deal with one fire at a time. We need to get Judge Parker back under control, so talk to Grade and make sure he didn't fuck anything up. Once this all dies down, we can deal with Fisher's grudge against Pulaski Senior."

Clay leaned forward to set the bottle down on the table. His fingers slid down the cool glass of the neck for a moment, and then he stood up.

"You're going to hand Grade over to them, aren't you?" he asked.

Ezra didn't exactly answer. He just set his bottle down right next to Clay's, close enough that the glass clinked together. Clay's brain glitched briefly, pushed apart under the pressure, and the table smeared from honeycomb-punched white metal to cheap, scarred-up plastic, the bottles from Carlsberg to unlabeled green glass bottles that were refilled every night in the back of the bar.

Old debts.

"Not if we can avoid it," Ezra said. "Just remember that I'm your best friend and your business partner, and like you said,

Grade is just someone you fuck sometimes. Now let's get out of here before we have to eat Fisher's fucking shitty cake."

DIRTY JOB

CHAPTER NINE

"This country is going to hell in a handbasket carried by feminist liberals," the man's voice ranted out of the speakers as the van's radio suddenly tuned in to a stray FM station. "They might say that what they want is—"

Grade flicked the radio off. Silence was better.

The sign for the Choke loomed on the side of the road as Grade took the bend tightly. At night the mascot was lit up in flickering orange neon, but by day the sexy chicken lady had to stand on her own merits.

Blocky bright red letters advertised:

Hot Women!!

Hot Water!

Hot Wings!!!

Grade wasn't exactly the target demographic for any of those, but he took the hard left the arrow directed him to into the Choke's parking lot. He pulled into an empty space, turned the engine off, and got out of his van. The Choke was open from four in the afternoon until lunchtime.

The daytime trade was, according to Dory, mostly there for the hot water and the hot wings. They also tipped for shit, which is why she never pulled the first or last shifts.

So at three in the afternoon, Grade could be pretty sure he wasn't going to run into her. Which was the point.

He headed toward the building. The lot was mostly empty, but a few cars were still parked outside. One of the managers would be here and some staff, getting the place ready to reopen and firing up some of those wings. The other cars—Grade glanced into one on the way by and saw a stoner-looking dude in his thirties or hard-worn twenties, passed out on the cranked-back front seat—were mostly patrons either still sleeping off the night before or here early to tie one on.

The big double doors that were the main entrance were chained shut. There were normal locks too, but some of the drunks needed the visual to work out why they weren't getting in. Grade cut around the side, past the blacked-out windows and the dumpsters that smelled of baby oil, chicken grease, and booze. He stopped at the fire door and hit the intercom, head tilted back so the camera over the door could see his face.

"Who the fuck are you?" an annoyed voice demanded.

"Dory Pulaski's brother," Grade said. "I need a word about some guy who's been bothering her."

The intercom snorted at him and cut out. He pressed the button again, held it down, and waited. After a long second, it crackled back to life.

"OK, look. You don't like your sister being a stripper. I get it, but—"

"That's her business," Grade said. "I just need to know about Verne."

There was a pause, and then the intercom cut out for a second time. Before Grade could jam his thumb back down on the button, the door popped open. He shoved it all the way open and went into the dimly lit corridor.

With no strippers to keep on track, the Choke's management saw no need to light up the backstage area. Grade paused for a second as he waited for his eyes to adjust and then followed the bass beat of music to the main bar of the Choke.

A woman in a tailored suit, leather suspenders pulled slanted in a *V* either side of her breasts, posed on a dais with the pole behind her and a selfie light in front of her. One of the bouncers had pulled a chair up and stood on it as he filmed her.

"TikTok," the man at the bar, his voice familiar from the intercom, said. He looked up from the books he was working on, columns of numbers marched down a lined page, and nodded at the stage. "I say all we need to do is flash some tit, but Sal says that it's all about the transition. I guess we'll find out when we see what goes viral."

Grade shrugged. "I wouldn't know," he said. "I'm not on social media."

That wasn't entirely true. Grade had a handful of accounts on most platforms, but that was business. He didn't interact, not as himself. Like tattoos, social media gave people way too many ways to identify someone. The little things that people didn't think to change about themselves: Coffee orders. Favorite podcasts. Hobbies and habits.

"And look what you're missing," the man said as he nodded at the stage.

Grade half turned to get an eyeful as the dancer peeled her shirt off, her body artfully splattered with gold.

"I think I'll live," he said.

"Your loss," the man said. He capped his pen, set it down in the crease of the book, and extended his hand. "Aidan Dunphy. And you're Dory's little brother?"

Grade tried not to sound annoyed by the need to correct that assumption. "I'm older than her."

Dunphy raised his eyebrows and looked Grade up and down.

"Huh," he said, turning his mouth down at the corners. "And she's never mentioned she hates you?"

"Why state the obvious?" Grade asked.

Dunphy smirked and sat back, his elbow braced against the bar. He was a solid, heavy-shouldered man with close-cropped salt-and-pepper hair and a slightly grayer beard. Old tattoos stretched over his knuckles as he picked up a glass of iced water to take a drink.

"So what do you want to know about Verne?" he asked.

"Where I can get in touch with him."

Dunphy set the glass down and wiped his mouth on the back of his hand. "You know what's funny? Someone just dropped his new address off this morning." He stretched over the bar and shuffled around for a second before he came up with a business card. There was a coffee stain on one side of it, and the corners were thumbed over. Dunphy held it out between his fingers and flicked the edge with his nail. "Here you go."

The Cargill County Sheriff's Department logo was printed on cheap card stock in smudged ink. Grade wasn't usually paranoid, but that seemed like the setup for an embarrassing end to his career. He didn't take the card; instead, he tilted his head to the side to read it.

"Deputy Paul Martin?" he read out.

"You want to see Verne, talk to him," Dunphy said. "He'll get you into the morgue."

When Grade didn't take the card, Dunphy shrugged and tossed it back behind the bar.

"What happened?" Grade asked.

"He died," Dunphy deadpanned.

"How?"

Dunphy shrugged and picked up his pen again. He pulled the cap off and set it to the side, next to the glass of water.

"Deputy Martin wasn't here to shoot the shit with me," Dunphy said. "But he was here because he knew Verne was a regular. Asked if he'd had any problems with any of the girls or other customers, so I'd guess he didn't die of natural causes."

That sounded like a safe bet.

"Had he?" Grade asked.

Dunphy shook his head. "No," he said. "Everyone liked Verne. He did some work for a couple of the girls—tracked down people who owed them money or exes who'd skipped out—and none of them had anything bad to say. He did his job, didn't charge over the odds, never offered to let them pay in kind. No one here had any problem with him. Well, except Dory, I guess. Hopefully it wasn't the sort you kill people over?"

He laughed at his own joke. Grade smiled along with him, but the problem was that Grade didn't know that. Not for sure. Maybe it was a coincidence that Verne had poked his nose into what happened to Tommy Pulaski and then turned up dead. And that he'd apparently been working on a no-win, no-fee deal that had gotten Dory her money back.

Or…

Or Verne had actually found something, decided not to tell Dory, and whatever it was had gotten him killed.

Call Grade a fatalist, but that sounded more likely to him.

"What did you want to talk to him about?" Dunphy asked, a hint of curiosity in his voice.

Grade shook his head. "I guess it doesn't matter now," he said with a shrug as he stepped back. "Good luck with TikTok."

Dunphy snorted and waved his hand dismissively. "Like I told Sal, people tip when their stomachs are full of chicken and they've got tits all up in their face. Not because she lip-synched to some old TV show."

Grade shrugged and turned to go.

"Hey." Dunphy stopped him. "You know if Dory has trouble with anyone, she just has to tell me. She's a good earner. The last thing we want is for her to get spooked and leave."

"She's pretty hard to spook," Grade said as he took another couple of steps away from the bar. "I… Verne had just offered to do some checks for her, private stuff, and I was worried he might be a con artist. Guess I misjudged him."

Dunphy shook his head. "Who knows," he said. "None of the girls he worked for had any complaints, but people can always surprise you."

He went back to his accounts, and this time Grade left without anyone stopping him. When he got out to the parking lot, Clay was waiting for him, propped up against the side of the van with a cigarette in hand.

Grade stopped mid-step, caught between whether to ask how Clay had found him or why he'd wanted to. He didn't have to pick. Clay pushed himself off the van—the outline of his shoulders left smudged into the dust caked on the white metal—and flicked the butt down onto the concrete between his feet. He ground it out under one foot, embers smeared over the concrete in a long curve. The sharp-edged man from the other night, in gray cotton and a tailored suit, was gone, and instead, the sleep-tangled curls, faded canvas jacket, and old jeans were back.

It would have been nice if that made him less distracting, but Grade had a specific type. This hit all his buttons.

"I've been looking for you," Clay said. "We need to talk."

§

"I told you," Grade said. "Never work with amateurs."

"Bit late for that," Clay said. He took the burgers from the girl in the food truck and handed her a couple of notes in trade. "Keep the change."

"It's never too late to say 'I told you so,'" Grade said. He held out his hand, and Clay gave him the Southern Fried Turkey Burger while he hung on to the cheeseburger and fries. "This is what amateurs do, they get *feelings* about the job, and that's when it gets messy."

The handkerchief of green space in the center of Sweeny was named Caplin Park, after the owner of the mining company that used to run the town. Like the school and the hospital, the park had been something to convince people that mining was a good job and would totally take care of their descendants too.

It had stood more or less ignored for years, except as a desire path to get somewhere better quicker, until the pandemic. The uptick in people who lingered had resulted in the addition of two new trash bins and a handful of picnic tables clustered around the statue of Caplin's rearing horse.

The statue used to be of Caplin *on* his horse, but he'd been broken off during protests when the mines closed up. Now all that was left were two stone legs in stirrups.

Grade grabbed a picnic table in front of the horse, under the granite hooves, and started to deconstruct the burger.

"I've killed plenty of people I had a real hard-on for," Clay said as he straddled the bench opposite. He set his plate down in front of him and picked at it, but most of his attention was on the park around them.

"You might want to keep that to yourself," Grade said. He found a pickle and set it aside. "Especially when you're talking to the guy you're fucking."

A lazy grin curled the corner of Clay's mouth as he tracked a couple with a screaming child across the perimeter of the park. He shifted focus as they cut across the road to go into the shop.

"I thought that's what you liked about me," he said. "That I was dangerous."

That one was hard to argue. Grade pulled the corner off his slab of turkey and dunked it in the hot sauce. He waved the slathered bit of meat in the air.

"Bad boys, sure," he said. "Actual psychopaths, not so much. If I was into that, I could have stayed in LA, locked up in someone's basement."

"I thought you didn't work with amateurs."

"No spree killers or serial killers," Grade corrected him. "As long as they do it for money, it's not my business if they enjoy it."

Clay snorted and pulled a bottle of water out of his pocket. He tossed it over the table. Grade caught it out of the air, the plastic slippery and cold in his hands, before it landed on his plate.

"If I tell you that you're right," Clay asked, "will you shut up?"

Grade twisted the cap off the water and thought about that for a second. He finally shrugged and took a long drink.

"I mean, sure." He set the bottle back down and wiped his hands on his thighs. "Not for long, but for a while."

Clay leaned over the table and took Grade's chin in his hand. If Grade had meant to go back on their deal, that was out the window. His thoughts scattered at the scrape of callused skin along his jaw, his throat too dry and sticky to get any words he did come up with out over his tongue.

"It seemed like a good idea at the time," Clay said.

Grade blinked and cleared his throat. A couple of times.

"I don't think that counts," he said.

"It's close enough," Clay said. Then he let go of Grade's face and stole a pickle off his plate. He crunched on it as he slouched back onto his side of the table. "And it doesn't matter. If we can't satisfy our, ah, amateur associate that their fat is well removed from the fire? She's going to go to Fisher and ask him to tidy up loose ends, and you don't want to be on Fisher's radar."

There was something about the way Clay said that last part that made Grade give him a curious look. It felt like it used to at school, when the teachers had been talking about him behind his back. Except he didn't think that this was about mandatory sessions with the school counselor.

"Maybe it wouldn't be such a bad thing," Grade said, to see Clay's reaction. "He might throw a few more jobs my way."

That would be a mixed blessing. Grade would take the money, but working for someone like Fisher could be restrictive. It was easy to go from "useful" to "knows too much" with just one job in an organization. Then even if they didn't get rid of him, well, Lexington was better than Sweeny, but he didn't want to spend the rest of his life there.

Clay thought about that for a second, then scratched his jaw. His nails scraped over a couple of days' worth of stubble.

"That's one outcome," he said. "Except I don't think you'd be able to deliver what Fisher wants from you."

"Why not?"

A smile twitched over Clay's mouth, and he shook his head. "Need to know," he said. "Just trust me and keep your head

down. I'll handle Fisher, and you tell me that you did a
bulletproof job and covered our associate's ass."

Grade spread greasy hands and then grabbed a napkin to
wipe them. "I can't do that," he said. "I told you that, and that
was before we found out that one of them was a district
attorney."

"She was fired."

"Yeah, because of a scandal," Grade said. "That's pre-loaded
interest in the case from the press, from the cops, from the DA's
office. It could play out in our favor—if someone decides it would
be better to get that swept back under the rug—or not. I can't
predict that. The best I can do is tell your associate to keep her
nerve and don't do anything to draw attention to herself."

Clay picked up his burger.

"It turns out she wants to retrieve the things you took from
the house," he said and then took a bite. He added, through the
mouthful of food, "Apparently, she thinks you'll get caught with
your hand in the stolen cookie jar and turn her in."

Grade pushed the plate away from him. "She can fuck off,"
he said. "I'm not going to put my neck on the line like that."

"But you could?" Clay asked. He pushed the plate back over
to Grade. "You still have it?"

Grade picked off a chunk of turkey from the burger and
shredded it absently as he considered that question. He finally
gave in and nodded.

"I could get it," he admitted. "But I'm not going to. I don't
expect much from the local deputies, but I'm not going to hand
them evidence either. Just in case."

"You don't have to," Clay said. "Just don't get rid of it. Not
yet. If our friendly neighborhood judge is really that intent on the
idea you'll flog an heirloom nipple piercing and get caught, we

can tell her we'll find a way to get rid of it all once the heat has died down."

Grade didn't like it. Placate a nervous client once, and they'd just wait until that hit wore off and be back for more. There were only so many compromises that could be made without undermining the job that was already signed off on.

Except he was just the subcontractor in this case. That meant it wasn't his call.

"You can tell her what you like," he said. "Just keep my name out of it. Fisher isn't the only one whose radar I want to stay off."

Clay finished his burger and crumpled the stained paper plate into a ball. "Make it worth my while and I'll think about it," he said.

"If you expect me to put out just because you bought me dinner," Grade said as he cleared up his side of the table, "you'll need to take me on a nicer date than this."

"Is that what this is?" Clay asked as he took the rubbish out of Grade's hands. "A date?"

Grade felt his ears burn. He tried to ignore it.

"It's a figure of speech."

"It really isn't," Clay said. "But you keep telling yourself that."

He walked away to dump the rubbish in one of the nearby bins. Grade rubbed the back of his neck and watched Clay go as he wondered if it had been a date.

Of course, the second part of that question was, did he *want* it to be a date?

Grade wasn't ready to think about that one, so he put the whole query back on ice. If he thought about it too much right now, the answer might result in him not getting laid. He could come back to it later—after Clay had pissed him off and he could be sure that the last thing he'd want is for this to have been a date.

Over the years, Grade had given up a lot of plans he had for his life, but getting the hell out of Sweeny—*again*—wasn't going to be one of them.

CHAPTER TEN

"YOU NEED TO learn to fucking listen," Ezra said. He jabbed his fingers against the side of Clay's head. "And use this."

"You want me to headbutt him next time?" Clay asked.

He pulled his T-shirt over his head, hissing in pain as the scars over his ribs pulled… and… No. That wasn't it. He didn't have any scars. Just bruises and maybe a broken rib. He probed his side absently with one hand to try and gauge the damage Reid's boot had done. It wasn't good. It could be worse.

"You don't have to take the fucking bait every time," Ezra said. "Play it smart."

Clay laughed and threw himself down on the cot. He bunched the thin pillows up behind his head. It hurt to laugh, but it hurt to breathe, too, so what the fuck.

"Fuck 'em," he said.

"Just keep your fucking head down," Ezra said. "Reid isn't going to forget this, and we need him. He's the one who knows the warlords, remember. He can walk us straight through."

He left.

Clay closed his eyes and fell into a doze.

Something woke him up

He opened his eyes and stared up into Reid's face. It was hard to tell which of them was more surprised. Probably Clay. From the smell of Reid's breath, he was too drunk to register what a fuckup he'd made in time.

"Get him," Reid spluttered as he threw himself down on top of Clay, an arm wedged up under his throat. "Hold him down."

Shadows moved around them in the tent, and Clay realized he might have been the fuckup here. He punched Reid in the side of the head and threw him off. Once the weight wasn't pinning him down, Clay rolled away from the bed and lunged for his kit.

His hand closed on nothing, and there were floorboards under his knees, not the ground cloth of the tent. Clay blinked himself awake and shook his head to clear the fog.

Here, not there. Now, not then.

Grade, not Reid? Fuck. That would solve all of Clay's problems in the worst goddamn way.

The fog clung on; his brain dragged like taffy between dream and groggy reality.

One of Reid's friends tackled him before he could grab his gun, her *arm around his throat as* she dragged him away from the bed. Military boots scuffed the floor as she scrabbled at her hip with the other hand.

Clay went limp. The sudden drag of deadweight on her muscles made her stagger and lose her grip. He got his hand up and grabbed one of her fingers—heavy leather gloves, well-fitted—and yanked it back until he heard it pop like a chicken bone.

She grunted behind clenched teeth as the pain hit her, but she managed to hang on.

"Hold him," a man ordered.

She tightened the chokehold and leaned back, her legs braced as she tried to let his weight strangle him. Another figure—the man—stepped forward with something black and boxy in one hand. Taser. Clay got his feet under him and twisted violently;

his thigh muscles tensed painfully as he arched his back. The contacts caught him on the thigh instead of the stomach.

It still hurt like fuck. His leg folded under him, the muscles corded and numb like dead wood under the skin, and he thrashed violently. He bit his tongue hard enough to taste blood...

The rope pulled back between Clay's teeth like a bit, his tongue raw as it scraped the top of it. Blood trickled down the back of his throat, salt and pennies.

"Hold the bastard still!" someone—Graham, from the last dregs of a speech impediment to his voice—blurted in a panic.

"He's seen us!" Lawrence said, her voice shrill and anxious. "What are you going to do?"

They were going to kill him, Grade realized with distant clarity.

They wanted him alive. For now, at least.

One leg was dead wood, but the rest of him still worked. Clay had been hit with a taser before. He was that sort of asshole. There was a knife strapped to the woman's ankle. He grabbed it and pulled it out of the sheath. The blade was short and broad, painted black except for a sickle of bright metal along the edge. It had a good weight to it.

Clay got his knee under him and slashed up with the knife. The woman had body armor on, he'd felt that in the struggle, but the joints were always the weak spot. People had to move. The blade cut through heavy canvas combat trousers and sliced the crease of her thigh deeper. Blood splattered out over his hand and down his arm. He pulled back and sliced at the other side. She managed to block him, both hands around his wrist, but it didn't matter.

The knife hadn't gotten the femoral artery, no blood gush, but it had sliced open the vein. She wouldn't be on her feet for long.

Clay rolled backward and used her grip on him to drag her with him. He got his good foot in her gut and flipped her over his head. She tumbled into the man with the Taser and fouled his footing. He cursed as he tried to untangle himself from her and keep his feet under him on the bloody floor.

Two.

No. Clay scrambled awkwardly up off the ground. His foot was still cramped up, the toes curled in painfully tight, but it held under his weight. He wiped the back of his hand across his mouth.

"Alexa, turn on lights," he said.

The spotlights in the ceiling flicked on and flooded the room. It made...

... *Reid turned his head away and squinted, his face gray and his nose smeared over his face like putty. Clay pulled the rope out of his mouth and spat on the ground...*

"Should have brought more people," he said.

He wasn't sure who he'd said that to.

Four. Three now. The woman on the floor didn't show any sign of getting up. She sprawled on her back, jaw set and one hand clutched to her thigh as blood seeped between her fingers.

"Put the knife down," the man with the Taser said. He tilted his head to the bed where another man knelt on Grade's chest, a knife to his throat. "Or we cut his throat."

Clay weighed his options. After a moment he shrugged and held his hands up. He let the knife drop, and it thunked into the ground next to his foot.

"Smart man," Taser said. He pointed at the bed with his chin. "Sit down."

Clay backed up and sat on the edge of the bed.

"You OK?" he asked over his shoulder.

Grade tilted his chin back and swallowed. The knife had sliced a paper-cut-thin line in his throat, and blood dripped down onto the bed. "I've been better," he said.

Taser pulled his hand down over his mouth and chin, exhaled raggedly, and then turned to the last member of the group.

"Patch Cisco up," he told him. "Get her ready for exfil."

Clay laughed. "Exfil. You got a fucking chopper coming in?" he asked. "Or you just play with your Action Men too much as a kid?"

Taser glared at him. He holstered his taser on his belt and bent down over Cisco. One hand gripped her upper arm with brief reassurance; then he unclipped the identical blocky plastic weapon from her hip. He walked over, bloody footprints left on the wood, and bent down to shove it against Clay's balls.

"Shut your mouth until I tell you to open it," he said. "When I ask you a question, you answer it, and we all go home happy. Don't, and I put 1000 volts through your cock. How much good do you think that will be to your boyfriend?"

Clay leaned back and braced his arms on the bed behind him. He grinned at Taser. "We're not dating," he said. "And it wouldn't kill him to do some of the work in bed."

"Fuck you," Grade said.

Clay jerked his head in that direction. "See? He says that, but he never follows through. All mouth."

Taser pulled a sour face. He hooked a finger at the man who had Grade pinned down and pointed at the bed next to Clay.

"Get him up here," he said.

The mattress bounced as the man got off the bed. He twisted his fingers in Grade's hair and dragged him, naked and half tangled in the sheet, down to sit next to Clay.

"His cock goes next," Taser said as he pointed at Grade. "So, are you going to tell us what we want to know?"

"Of course," Grade said.

"Don't fall for that," Clay told him. "Even if you tell them the truth right off the bat, they're going to torture you anyhow to see if you stick to the story. Right?"

Taser laughed softly as he glanced over at one of his companions. He had a tattoo on his neck, just visible between his camo paint and his collar. It looked like a Celtic cross. Clay filed that away for reference as he tried to weigh up who he was dealing with.

They had training. It could be military, but Clay doubted it. It felt more cobbled together than that.

"The other option is that I start torturing you now," he said. "What do you have to lose?"

The man who had been designated as the nurse slapped a surgical bandage against the woman's thigh. He hooked his arms under her and levered her up onto his shoulder as she bit her fist to stifle the groans. Definitely not military, then, not with that lift. He headed for the door.

Meanwhile, the last member of the team turned Clay's room over. He dragged out drawers and emptied them, pulled clothes out of the closet, and used a knife to carve a gash into the seat of the leather chair in the corner of the room. Stuffing was pulled out and discarded on the floor.

"What do you want?" Clay asked.

The hit of adrenaline had cleared his head, stripped back the fog and the noise. Sex and violence, those were the only times that Clay felt like he wasn't swimming against the current of his own brain. Clarity in short, sharp shocks.

If it weren't for the fact he could hear the unevenness in Grade's breathing and the slight tremble in the arm nudged up against Clay's, this would be a good night.

"Where is it?" Taser asked.

"I don't know," Grade said. His voice cracked with frustration. "I never knew. It's nothing to do with me."

Taser backhanded him. The crack of contact was loud enough to make Clay start in surprise and knock Grade off the bed. He sprawled on the floor, his skin pale. He didn't move for a second, and then he propped himself up on his elbow, one hand pressed against the side of his face.

The hot flash of rage pushed Clay to his feet. He took a step toward Taser and stopped as the man pulled a gun out of the holster and pointed it at Clay's forehead. They stared at each other for a second, and then Taser smiled and shifted the gun to point at Grade's back.

"Sit down," he ordered.

Clay took that one step back, but stayed on his feet.

"Fisher told us to deal with this," Clay said. "I'm dealing with it. This wasn't necessary."

Grade pushed himself up into a sitting position. The skin on his cheekbone was split, blood dribbled down his bloody jaw, and he had a fat lip, already shaded blue and bruised.

"Fisher?" he asked

That could wait. Clay made eye contact with Taser.

"You can just walk away from this," he said. "None of us are going to the sheriff's department, are we?"

Taser made an annoyed sound. "I'm here to do a job, not take a walk," he said. "Where the fuck is the laptop?"

That was unexpected.

There had been eyes on them earlier in the park. Clay had assumed they'd been Fisher's backup plan, just in case Clay went with that bad decision after all. He'd not even been mad. It was a fair enough concern. Clay had a rep for going rogue, even before Grade came on the scene.

It was like that old proverb, though. When you had too many enemies, any of them could be the one fucking you over right now.

Something like that, anyhow.

"Last chance to just back off," Clay said. "No harm, no foul."

Taser twisted his mouth into a reluctantly admiring smile as he shook his head. "You've got balls," he said. "But we both know that you'd come after me. Because you think you're a crazy fucker, and that's what crazy fuckers do. Right?"

Clay shrugged one shoulder. "Multiple doctors have diagnosed me as a crazy fucker," he said. "There's no 'think' involved. The rest of it… you're not wrong. It turns out I like Grade's face unfucked up."

"Don't feel too bad," Taser said. "The boss said no loose ends. This is always how it was going to go down. You just have to decide how hard it's going to be."

The fourth member of the team kicked the slashed chair over. "It's not here," he said. "Sundance checked downstairs, but he didn't find anything either. He said that Cisco was in a bad way, though."

Code names. Clay doubted they'd lead anywhere—who'd be that stupid?—but he made a note anyhow. Taser nodded his acknowledgment of that and stalked over to Grade. He grabbed a handful of hair and yanked Grade up until he could press the gun against the nape of his neck. What color there was in Grade's face had drained away, the stray freckles over his cheekbones stark. His eyes, the socket of one shadowed in bruise tones, were flinty green.

"Tell me where the fucking laptop is," he said. "Or your cleaner ain't going to be able to clean his own ass."

Grade swung his arm back and drove the knife he'd pulled out of the floorboards into Taser's arm. The blade hit the body-armor greaves and skidded but caught in the gap between sleeve and cuff. Grade twisted the knife before he yanked it free, gagging at the sight of blood, and Taser fumbled the gun, then dropped it.

Clay threw himself forward. He grabbed the gun out of midair, just before he landed shoulder first on the wooden floor and rolled back up onto his knees. The gun settled easily into his hand. Mass production meant it felt familiar even though he'd never held this one before. He pointed it at Taser for a heartbeat, then pivoted on his knee and shot the fourth man in the head as he went for his gun.

The man gawped at Clay for a moment, his eyes wide and mouth slack as blood dripped down his forehead and into his eyes. Then he went down like a puppet whose strings had been cut, limp and awkward.

Clay got to his feet and turned in one smooth motion to point the gun at Taser.

"Who do you work for?" he asked.

Taser held up one hand to ward him off. His other arm was tucked in close to his body, the fingers on his hand curled into his palm like dead spider legs.

"I can't tell you that, even if I wanted to," he said. "We don't take names, just money and the job. Look, like you said, we can walk out of here. You won. Fair play."

"Shut up," Clay said. He pointed at the bed with the gun. "Sit down."

Taser licked his lips and glanced at the door, then at his dead friend. He sat down on the edge of the bed. Clay looked over at Grade as the other man scrambled to his feet and grabbed his discarded jeans to pull back on.

"You OK?" Clay asked.

Grade nodded, thought about it, and turned it into a shrug. He reached up to gingerly poke at his cheekbone with his thumb.

"Nothing broken," he said.

"See?" Taser said. "Looks like you two fuckers came out ahead. I'm down two members of my team, and all you've got is a split lip."

Clay ignored him.

"Take the taser off him," he told Grade.

Grade did as he was asked. With the gun pointed at his head, Taser didn't try anything funny. He handed the blocky plastic gun to Grade, who brought it back over to Clay. He tested the weight of it in his off hand.

"What was the job?" he asked. "Get the laptop? Kill us?"

Taser looked away and licked his lips again. It was a brutal tell. He'd be a shit poker player.

Clay's nose was bunged up with dried blood as he limped out of his tent; the doubled length of bloody rope still dangled from one hand. Despite what she'd said about "not being a part of this" when she'd tapped out of the beatdown, Lawrence hadn't gone far. She was still outside, her nails raw from being picked at, and she blanched when she saw Clay.

He dropped the rope and got ready to say something smart-assed about sitting on the fence. Before he could get it, someone started shouting on the other side of camp, where Ezra's tent was.

"We just wanted to teach you both a lesson," Lawrence blurted out.

"Save it," Clay snarled at her as he headed toward the sounds of alarm.

Clay handed the gun to Grade, grabbed Taser by the throat, and shoved him onto the bed. He straddled the other man's thigh, knee braced on the mattress, and shoved the Taser into the soft grease-covered skin under his jaw.

"How many did you send after Ezra?"

"I can call them off," Taser said. "You just need—"

Clay shoved the taser into his mouth before he could finish that sentence. Panic widened the man's eyes, and he squirmed violently as he tried to get away. Clay tightened his grip and waited for him to gag himself out.

"How many?" he asked again.

Taser held up his good hand with two fingers extended. Then he jabbed them at Clay's eyes as he bucked under him in a desperate attempt to get away. If he hadn't done that, Clay didn't know if he'd have pulled the trigger or not. Although—he remembered the crack of a hand against Grade's face—he probably would have. Clay had never been a man to bluff.

The trigger clicked, and 1000 volts plugged into the wet flesh under Taser's tongue. His eyes rolled back in his head, and his whole body arched up in a bow-tight convulsion as the charge poured through him. His heels drummed against the floor, and his jaw clenched so tight that the plastic cracked as his teeth clamped down on it.

Some of his teeth too.

Clay let go of the trigger and let Taser flop bonelessly onto the bed, still twitching as his muscles tried to deal with the jolt they'd gotten. Drool spiked with blood dribbled out of his mouth and onto the bedspread.

"Is he dead?" Grade asked.

"Not yet," Clay said grimly as he straightened up. There was a warm, wet patch under his knee where the man had lost control of his bladder. He made a mental note to order himself a new mattress and turned to Grade. "Stay here. Call Ezra and see if you can get through."

Grade nodded while Clay quickly changed the cartridge on the Taser and then swapped it with Grade for the gun. There was a pair of old sweats tipped out of the laundry basket, and he grabbed them to pull them quickly on. The thin material clung to his damp skin as he pulled them up his legs and left them slung low around his hips.

He grabbed Taser by the front of his Kevlar vest and dragged him off the bed. The man hit the floor with a heavy thud but didn't even groan. His head hung laxly from his neck as Clay dragged him over the bloody, slippery floor and out onto the landing.

While they'd been upstairs, the last walking member of Taser's team had turned over the ground floor of Clay's house. The couch had been ripped open, holes bashed in the walls, and the TV smashed and tipped over onto the floor.

"No sign of it down here," the man yelled without looking up as he emptied the trash onto the floor and kicked through it. "Did either of them talk?"

"Most people would say you can't shut me up," Clay said conversationally from the top of the stairs. The man jerked his head up and stared at Clay in shock for a heartbeat before he went for his gun. He was too slow. Clay dropped his aim and fired a bullet into the ground between his feet, gouging a splintered hole into the polished floorboards. "Try again and I'll put one in your throat."

Clay dropped Taser's limp body and kicked him down the stairs. The man tumbled down the steps and landed at the bottom, arms and legs bent at painful angles. For a moment, Clay thought the fall had finished him off, but then he coughed out a ragged exhale and spluttered blood down his cheek.

The last man standing went to bolt for the door. Clay rolled his eyes and shot the ground again, this time close enough to the guy's foot that it took a chunk out of the heavy rubber sole of his boot. It made the man flinch and freeze in place.

"Don't fucking move," Clay warned as he came down the stairs. He stepped over Taser and walked over to the last man, gun still in his hand. The guy swallowed hard and went to say something. Clay didn't want to hear it. "Shut up."

The man did. His teeth clicked audibly as he closed his mouth. Clay took the gun out of his holster, stepped back, and thumbed the button to eject the magazine. It dropped onto the floor, and he kicked it away from him. Then he nodded over to Taser.

"Take him and get the fuck out of my house," Clay said. "Count of three."

Indecision froze the team's last man for a second. Clay pointed the gun at the man's head.

"One," he said. "Two."

In the twenty or so years that Clay had been threatening people for fun and money, no one had ever called his bluff on that. Today was no different. The man bolted forward, grabbed Taser under the arms, and dragged him backward out of the house. The last Clay saw of them was Taser's boots as they bounced out the door.

Clay waited for a minute until he heard the sound of an engine as it revved hard to peel out of his drive. He took a second and then loped up the stairs to stalk back into the bedroom, tossing both guns in the direction of the bed.

"I called," Grade said. He held up the phone like he thought Clay might want to see the evidence. "I couldn't get through."

Clay grabbed a T-shirt off the floor, ignored the wet splatter of blood soaked into it, and pulled it on. He stamped his feet into his boots, laces left to trail, and then threw Grade's jacket at him.

"You're coming with me," he said. "Come on."

Grade pulled the jacket on and then hesitated, arms halfway down the sleeves, as he nodded toward the dead man ruining the flooring at the other side of the room.

"What about him?"

Clay grabbed his jacket. "Tomorrow's problem," he said. "Come on."

They took the car. Grade braced himself in the passenger seat, his thighs flexing when he tried to brake because Clay didn't. Once they hit a straight stretch of road, Clay fished his phone out of his jacket pocket and called Ezra.

No one answered.

"He could have been lying," Grade offered after a second. "He might have thought it would buy him time."

"Yeah," Clay said. He killed the call and put in one to his favorite bought and paid for dirty cop, Deputy Jones. The Bluetooth kicked in as Jones answered.

"Not a good time," he said.

Clay snorted. "You've no idea," he said. "If anyone puts in a call about a disruption at my house? There isn't. Got it?"

"I can't control who gets tapped by dispatch."

"Not my problem," Clay said. "Do it."

He hung up and tossed Grade the phone. "Keep trying Ezra," he said and put his foot down on the gas.

DIRTY JOB

CHAPTER ELEVEN

THIRTY MINUTES.

Give or take. That's how long it would take Grade to render Ezra's body down, from the first cut to loading him in the back of the van. He'd worked it out a couple of times. The most time-consuming part would be peeling the tattoo off Ezra's back.

Proper disposal would take longer.

But Grade wasn't going to put that estimation to the test. Not tonight, anyhow.

Watered-down blood dripped down the back of Ezra's neck and stained the collar of his T-shirt as he paced angrily across his living room, a bag of peas pressed to his skull. Bloody welts ringed both wrists, and his left hand was swollen and discolored.

"My kids could have been here," Ezra said. "Do you get that? My *fucking* kids."

Clay handed him a glass of bourbon, and Ezra tossed it back in one. Then he swore and grimaced as he shifted the peas gingerly. He looked queasy as he stopped mid-stalk to lean his elbow on the oak island in the middle of the kitchen.

"That was a fucking mistake," he said as he breathed raggedly through clenched teeth.

Clay took the glass out of Ezra's hand.

"Stop whining," Clay said. He gave Ezra two pain pills. "You've had worse, and the kids *weren't* here."

"Fuck you," Ezra said. He dry-swallowed the pills and straightened up. "They could have been. *My* kids. I'm going to fucking kill someone."

Grade poked the corpse on the floor with the toe of his sneaker. The man's head lolled limply on a twisted neck.

"Else," he corrected Ezra. When that got him a glare, he shrugged. "When you're the cleanup crew, clarity on the numbers involved matters."

Ezra tried to point at him, but his hand didn't work. With a frustrated curse, he chucked the peas into the sink, where they landed with a mushy thud, and waved his good hand at Grade.

"You can shut up," he said. "Until we know this isn't your fault, I don't want to hear a word out of you."

"Give me your hand," Clay said. He grabbed for Ezra's wrist.

"Fuck you," Ezra repeated as he jerked his arm out of reach. He pulled the sleeve back and gestured at the jagged raised scar that ran down the inside of his forearm. "Last time you patched me up, this is what you left me with."

"Man up," Clay said.

This time he got hold of Ezra's hand and pulled it out straight so he could look at it under the lights. He pressed his thumbs between the knuckles and along the back, and Ezra's knees nearly buckled as the color drained from his face.

"What did they use?" Clay asked. "A hammer?"

"Butt of a gun," Ezra said. "Old school. Well?"

"You need to go to the ER," Clay said. He let Ezra reclaim his hand.

"I don't keep you around to tell me the obvious," Ezra said. "Just splint it up for now."

"It won't get better," Clay warned him.

"I've had worse," Ezra reminded him flatly.

"Fuck it," Clay said with a shrug. "It's your funeral."

He turned away to get the first aid kit from the top of the fridge. Ezra grabbed the bottle of bourbon and stuck it under one arm so he could wrestle the top off with one hand. The next shot he took straight from the bottle.

"I'm not fucking happy about this," he said.

"We got that," Clay said. "Wasn't exactly the round two I was planning on having tonight either. Put your hand down."

Ezra put his hand flat on the table.

"One," Clay started the countdown as he took hold of a crooked index finger. "Two—"

He yanked it straight. It made a hollow gritty sound that made Grade's stomach churn, the taste of blood replaced with bile in the back of his mouth.

Ezra yelped, slammed the bourbon bottle down on the countertop, and swore thickly. Fresh sweat beaded on his forehead as he doubled over and breathed raggedly.

"What the fuck happened to three?"

"You ask that every time," Clay said. "Ready?"

Ezra shook his head. He straightened up, tossed back another glug of bourbon, and then nodded. Grade gagged and looked away, but he still *heard* it as Clay did a DIY set of Ezra's little finger.

"I figured Fisher," Ezra said.

"Same." Clay started to splint Ezra's fingers. "But we've not given him any reason to come after us—I didn't even piss in his pool—and why the hell would he suddenly fixate on some laptop? That wasn't what he wanted from us."

"No," Ezra said. He wiped sweat out of his eyes on the sleeve of his T-shirt and nodded to the corner of the room. The remains of an HP lay cracked open on the tiles, the screen smashed with the heel of a boot. "I gave them mine, 'cause why the fuck not. What do I care if Fisher knows what porn I download? That crazy shithead probably cracks one off to *Shark Week* repeats. That wasn't what they wanted. It was a—"

"A MacBook Pro," Grade said. "Thirteen inch."

"Yeah, length of my cock," Ezra said sardonically. He broke off to suck his breath in through his teeth as Clay relocated a knuckle. "Fuck. That how you touch your boyfriend's cock?"

"If my cock was that color, I'd go to the ER," Grade said.

"Whatever," Ezra said. "So they told you the same thing."

Clay tied off the strapping and turned to look at Grade. "No," he said. "They never got round to that. Which begs the question—"

"Melanie Ledger," Grade said. "That was her laptop, the one I took from her office. MacBook Pro, with a Bellarmine sticker on the front."

Ezra worked his jaw from one side to the other, making the joint pop. Then he grimaced and turned to Clay.

"Deal with your fucking boyfriend," he said, pointing at Grade with the bourbon bottle. "I would, but I'd fucking kill him."

He slammed the bourbon down on the island and stalked over to the fridge to get another bag of frozen vegetables.

Grade held up both hands. "I was paid to stage a crime scene. I staged a crime scene," he said. "None of the stipulations I was given involved a laptop. How was I supposed to know it was important?"

"Well, it obviously fucking was," Ezra snapped. He sank down onto the floor and just stuck his hand into the freezer drawer. After a second, he tilted his head back against the door. "Could still be Fisher."

"Fisher doesn't need to hire heavies," Clay said. "He's got them on tap. Plus, why let us leave Lexington yesterday? His people were all over the place. If he wanted to know what we'd done with the laptop, he could have just hung us upside down in the pool."

Ezra scowled and rubbed the back of his neck with his good hand.

"That leaves one fucking awkward candidate, then," he said. "Goddamn it. She's a sitting judge. We can't touch the bitch."

He pulled his hand out of the deep freeze and slammed the door shut with his elbow. Clay picked up the bourbon bottle, wiped the mouth of it on his T-shirt, and downed a swig.

"She killed two people at her own party," he said. "Whatever is on that laptop, it can touch her. Somehow. Grade said he could get it back if we needed it. Now we need it."

Grade hesitated. That was another departure from standard operating procedures, and that hadn't paid off well for him so far. But Clay was right. If Parker had sent people to kill them, this was their only leverage.

"Give me a couple of hours," he said. "Once it's light."

"And us?" Ezra asked. He held up his hand and grimaced. "I don't think I could fit my thumb up my ass to sit on it right now, if that was your plan."

"We'll see if we can work out why Ledger and Collymore had to die."

§

The red-and-blue flicker of the light bar in the rearview mirror made Grade's shoulders tighten. Then the siren squawked once, and the driver stuck a hand out of the window to wave him over.

Grade pulled onto the side of the road, killed the engine, and sat back in the driver's seat. He hung his hands over the steering wheel, fingers relaxed, as he watched the deputy's patrol car swing in behind him.

The passenger side door opened, and a woman in an expensive suit got out. She closed the door behind her and stood for a second before she walked along the verge, unsteady in her heels, to tap on Grade's window. When Grade didn't immediately lower it, the woman smiled thinly and gestured back to the patrol car. The driver got out.

Shit.

Grade's MO was to avoid the cops when he could. Nothing good ever came of talking to them, and he'd seen plenty of people end up in jail because they ran their mouth to the wrong cop, assuming they were too dumb to catch on. That didn't mean he was worried about it. The van was clean, roadworthy, and Grade hadn't been speeding. There was nothing a cop could pull him in on.

This was different. It wasn't official, and that meant he didn't know the rules of engagement. He'd just have to kick it off on the assumption that getting his windows broken in wouldn't give him an advantage.

He leaned over and rolled the window down.

"Mr. Pulaski?" the woman said. "I'm Judge Charity Parker, and I want a word. Somewhere more comfortable."

Grade absently rubbed his cheekbone. He could feel the raised, rough texture of the scabbed-over skin. "That doesn't sound like a request," he said.

"It is," the woman assured him. "Until it isn't."

Of course. Grade pulled the keys out of the ignition and got out of the car.

"That's the right call," the woman said. "Come on."

She walked back to the car. As they approached, the deputy opened the back seat door for Grade. He hesitated but didn't see any other options, so he reluctantly climbed in. It smelled like Febreze and piss.

"Not your first time in one of these, I take it?" Parker asked as she got in the front.

"What makes you say that?" Grade asked.

Parker looked at him in the rearview mirror. "I looked at your juvie record," she said. "Breaking and entering? At fourteen. You're lucky that the family decided not to press charges. Why was that? You were a cute boy. Did you whore yourself out of a free pass?"

Grade sat back and buckled himself in. "They owed my mom money," he said. "That's why I broke in. If it went to court, the whole town would have found out. And while they didn't care if people thought they wouldn't pay the help, the fact they *couldn't* was something else altogether."

Charity chuckled as the deputy started the car. "Most people would be offended that I called them a whore, but I suppose when your sister is one, the sting wears off."

Silence.

It dragged on until they'd pulled back onto the road. Grade could feel the expectation in the air. She wanted him to bite back, to mouth off, but he wasn't sure why. It could be for her own satisfaction, or maybe she wanted to goad him into saying something she could use against him. Either way, he held his tongue.

The car drove along in silence until the buzz of Charity's phone interrupted it. She pulled it out of her pocket, glanced at the screen, and sighed heavily. Then she took the call.

"Benny," she said. "Sweetheart, now is not the time. I'm busy. Someone made a mess at work, and I have to clean it up. Yes."

Grade shifted position on the worn-down-to-the-springs upholstery. "What do you think would happen if I started screaming that I was being kidnapped?" he asked.

The deputy didn't look around at him. "I'd pull over," he said, "and beat you to death."

"That's what I figured," Grade said. He looked out the window as they reached the hairpin turn at the top of the road. Sweeny was spread out below them and looked the best it probably could in the morning sunlight. "I fucking hate this town."

Charity took the phone away from her face for a second to look around at him. "Don't we all," she said.

§

The pullout looked different in daylight.

A stray evidence tag had been left stuck to the ground next to the bloody stain on the concrete, and tabs of police tape fluttered in the air where they'd been cut off the barrier. Empty cups of coffee piled up in the single trash bin.

Grade walked over and looked down the mountain.

"It's quite the drop," Charity said. "It'd probably kill you, although the last person who took the trip was already dead."

Grade turned around and sat down on the barrier.

"What's this about?"

"I think you know."

"I think he's a cop, and you're a judge," Grade said, "so only an idiot would admit knowing anything."

Charity nodded and dropped her phone into her purse. "Fair enough," she said. "What if I admit that I paid you to get rid of two dead bodies?"

"I'd think that audio recordings can be edited," Grade said.

"That's going to make this conversation unnecessarily difficult."

"This isn't a conversation."

"You earned those skipped grades, didn't you," Charity said. "You're right. This is an offer, a one-time-only deal that you'll take. Because you're a smart boy, and you know how much influence someone like me has in a shithole like this."

Grade braced his hands against his thighs. "I know that someone like you has to be in a shithole like this to *have* influence," he said. "That's why you've never left Sweeny, right?"

She smiled. "You've done your research."

"No," Grade said. This was indulgent. He knew that. There was nothing to be gained by insulting Charity, but he'd had a bad night. "I just know people like you. I've seen them my whole life. Just smart enough to know that anywhere else, there's smarter."

She slapped him across his face.

That made her the second person to do that in twenty-four hours. Grade sat for a moment, his head turned to the side, as he licked blood from his reopened lip. Maybe he'd spent too much time with Clay.

"Was that the offer?" he asked.

Charity waved off the deputy when he started over, and rubbed her hand. "I want the laptop," she said. "Get it back to me and I'll give you enough money to put Sweeny in your rearview."

"I prefer a concrete offer," Grade said. "That's the sort of wording that could mean a lot or just enough for one full tank of gas."

"Ten grand."

"I could move to Lexington," Grade said. He stood up. They were probably about the same height, but in heels, Charity was taller than him. "I want two hundred grand."

She laughed at him.

"You think a lot of yourself."

"I do," Grade admitted. "But that's nothing to do with the amount. If you want me to do this, you need to make it worth my while. A hundred grand would be enough to get me back to California, give me a bit of a buffer. The rest is compensation for the fact I could never come back to Kentucky and the hit my reputation would take if it ever got out."

Charity looked him up and down. "You're a cold little bastard," she said.

"Practical."

"Deal," she finally said. "Get me the laptop. You'll have your ticket out of here. Don't wait too long."

She started to walk away.

"Why not offer this deal to Clay?" he asked. "Or Ezra?"

Charity turned around and looked at him. "Because you can be bought for two hundred grand," she said. "All they'd call that would be a down payment on a loan I'd never pay off. They'd never go away. I already know how that works. You'll take your money, though, and fuck off. And if you ever try to use what you know against me, I know where your family lives, and two hundred grand isn't enough for a fresh start for all of you, is it."

Grade stared at her for a second. Then he smiled thinly.

"You're a good judge of character," he said.

Charity looked sour for a moment. "Not always," she said. "But I think you and I have an understanding."

She gave him a brief nod and then headed back to the patrol car. It drove away and left Grade on the side of the road.

"See, I don't think you understand me at all," Grade said aloud as he watched the patrol car disappear. "But I think I've got a good handle on you."

§

"How did she know who I am?" Grade asked, his phone held against his ear by his shoulder as he hunted under the van's passenger side seat for a bottle of water he'd left there a couple of days before. The long walk back here from the viewpoint had sucked. His fingers bumped the warm plastic, and he pulled it out, giving it a shake to check if there was more than a mouthful left. He sat down on the edge of the door, twisted the top off, and took a drink. It had that old plastic taste that leeched out of the bottle. "That wasn't the deal. There wasn't supposed to be any contact between me and *your* client."

Clay was quiet for a moment.

"A lot of people would think better of speaking to me like that," he said.

"I know. I've met them," Grade said. "The difference is you don't want to fuck them."

"I don't want to fuck you either right now," Clay said.

"Please," Grade said dismissively. "The woman who hired thugs to kill us knows where I live and where my sister works. I can't—I *can't*—put Dory in the middle of my shit again."

He waited for Clay's answer as he stared at the concrete road between his feet. The sun was hot on the back of his neck.

"Ezra told her we had someone who could clean up her mess," Clay said after a moment. "Nothing else. But Charity has been in Fisher's pocket a long time, she knows people, and people talk. Buchanan made a splash."

People did. Word of mouth was how Grade got a lot of his jobs. Around here, at least. The Cargill County criminal fraternity were not terminally online. At one of the biker jobs, Grade had actually found paper-and-ink soft porn. As if that sort of stuff wasn't made for a wipe-clean hand-held device.

"I suppose," he conceded reluctantly.

"What did she want?" Clay asked.

"Same as you," Grade said. "For me to get the laptop back."

"Yeah? No jumping the queue. What did she offer you?"

"Two hundred grand," Grade said.

"Fuck," Clay said. "I'd probably take that deal."

"I doubt I'd ever see the money," Grade said. "She either had me followed from your house, or she has a tracker in the car. Either way, I'd bet on her plan being for me to lead her people straight to the laptop, and then they make sure I have an accident."

"So?"

Grade hesitated. He didn't work well with others, never had. It made him squirm to think about asking someone to do something he knew, in his heart, he could do better. On the other hand, he wasn't too fond of the idea of someone shoving him into a hole and leaving him there, either.

So maybe he could get through it this once.

"Harry?" he asked. "If I tell him where it is, he could maybe head out there to retrieve it with no one the wiser."

"You've got his number," Clay said. "Tell him I said he's to do what you tell him. And Grade?"

"Yeah?"

Clay hesitated for a moment. "Dory will be OK," he said. "I'll send some guys to keep an eye on her."

"Thanks," Grade said. He finished the water, tossed the empty bottle back in the car, and rubbed his hand through his sweaty hair. "I hate that people know how to get to me now I'm back here. In LA, no one knew I even had a family, never mind cared about them."

"To be fair, most people in Sweeny would still be surprised to find out you cared," Clay said dryly. "You don't scream family values."

Grade hung up on him.

DIRTY JOB

CHAPTER TWELVE

"ARE YOU SURE you can trust your boyfriend?" Ezra asked as he clumsily pulled his grimy, bloodstained shirt over his head. Fresh bruises decorated his torso, his abdomen dark and tender looking. "Parker waved a lot of money under his nose, and he's a greedy little shit."

Clay tucked the phone in his pocket. "Are you still bitter that he won't give you a discount? I'm the one fucking him."

"Does that get you twenty percent off?" Ezra asked as he balled the T-shirt up and tossed it into the bin. "Because I didn't know there were perks involved."

Clay shook out the shirt he'd grabbed from upstairs and held it out. "Keep pushing," he said. "I'm just waiting for the right jibe to bring up your ex."

"Like there's anything you can say about Janet that I've not already said?" Ezra asked. He clenched his teeth as he pulled the shirt on, sweat on his upper lip as he had to twist and shrug. "And most of them she'd agree with."

"No, I mean the one you liked," Clay said. "Pretty boy Paul."

Ezra gave Clay a dirty look. "Fuck you," he said. "You really want to do this instead of trying to find out what the hell is going on?"

"You tell me," Clay said. "You started it."

Ezra pulled a dour face as he tried to button the shirt one-handed. "Fine," he said. "Call it a draw."

Clay let Ezra struggle until it stopped being funny. Then he stepped in to feed the buttons through the holes, the cotton crisp under his fingers.

"Two guys," he said. "And they got the jump on you. There was a time that wouldn't have happened."

Ezra shrugged, visibly regretted it, and stepped back before Clay buttoned him all the way into his collar. He grabbed the jacket from the back of the door and pulled it over one arm, the other side left draped over his shoulder.

"Yeah, and that's why I'm divorced," Ezra said. "I have kids twice a week, a dog when Janet doesn't want it to see her hooking up, and I've never scared them. None of them flinch if they break something or slam the door. If they get scared at night, they come in and jump in bed with me without worrying I'll slap 'em into a wall. That's worth not being as sharp as I used to be."

He held up his field-bandaged hand and turned it over to check it from all sides.

"Most of the time," he added with a grimace.

They headed toward the back door. Clay got there first and unlocked it. He nudged it open with his shoulder.

"You're getting old, too," he said as Ezra stepped past him. "Can't forget that."

Ezra gave him a dirty look. "Shut up and get in the car," he said. "You're going to have to drive."

He clumsily pulled the keys from his pocket and tossed them to Clay, who grabbed them out of the air before they hit him in the chest.

"Who first?" he asked. "Hawes or Verne?"

It had to be one or the other. Lawyer or private investigator. Everyone else on the payroll was more of a blunt instrument.

"You heard me," Ezra said as he gingerly pulled himself into the passenger seat of the Range Rover. "Between Fisher and the fact she's a judge, there's not much we can do to Charity unless we can take one—preferably both—of those things away. So Hawes first. She said she'd meet us at the Slap. Besides, Verne isn't answering his fucking phone."

§

"Charity Parker," Vera Hawes said as she got up from behind Ezra's desk to give him his seat back. She was sixty years old and six feet tall, her hair cut in a sedate bob and dyed what she liked to call fuck-you fuchsia. Her legal career had started at twenty-one, took a thirty-year hiatus, and then she'd picked it up again after her husband killed himself rather than be convicted of money laundering. About the same time that Ezra and Clay had needed civilian legal counsel for the first time. She wasn't the best lawyer in the world, but she didn't have to be. If she couldn't find dirt on someone, it was because she already knew it. "Your enemies are coming up in the world."

"What can I say," Ezra said as he lowered himself into the leather chair with a wince. "I'm a social climber."

She snorted and walked over to the drinks cabinet.

"You look like you need this," she said as she got out a bottle of whiskey. She poured a glass and then turned around to use it to gesture at Ezra. "Don't suppose there's any chance the cops beat the shit out of you after an illegal traffic stop?"

Clay grabbed a chair from the corner of the room and pulled it up to the desk.

"He wasn't driving," he said.

Vera looked at him and sniffed. "So the stop would have been righteous," she said as she handed the whiskey to Ezra. That was fair enough; Clay could admit that. "Come on, boys. You know all I want in life is to be an ambulance chaser. Criminal law is a pain in the ass."

Ezra sat back.

"No crimes have been committed—"

"That you have to know about," Clay added as he sprawled out in the chair, his feet kicked up onto Ezra's desk.

"All we need to know is what we asked you about. Any dirt on Charity and any connection between her and Melanie Ledger," Ezra said. He nodded to Clay's feet. "And if you push his fucking feet off my desk, I'll give you a bonus."

Vera grabbed hold of Clay's jeans, down near his shins, and lifted his feet off the desk. She let them drop to the floor—with a thunk that Clay felt in his ankles—and brushed the spot on the desk off so she could perch her hip on it.

"It would have saved time," she said, "if you'd told me that was one and the same thing. Melanie Ledger was fired two years ago because the district attorney wanted the press to shut the fuck up about the whole jailhouse informant scandal that had blown up."

Clay hung his arm over the back of the chair. "We got that from the news."

"It was bullshit," Vera said. "My bestie in the DA's office says that everyone knew it. Ledger was a solid DA, but she didn't make any waves and never showed any spark. A workhorse, every office needs them. Right? Up until she was in court before Judge Parker, prosecuting some guy for beating the living shit out of his own mother. Parker threw every roadblock she could into the prosecution: Disallowed witnesses, upheld the *flimsiest* objection from the other side, and pushed for Ledger to offer mom-beater a deal."

"Who was the kid?" Clay asked.

"Why? So you can give him a slap if you meet him?" Vera asked. "Feel free. Tomas Grannick."

Clay hesitated for a second as he tried to place the name. Then he gave it up as a bad job—his brain hated logging names of people he needed to remember, so he wasn't going to remember some random kid—and looked over at Ezra.

"I don't know why I asked either," he said. "You?"

Ezra nodded. "Later," he said.

Vera glanced between them. "Good call. That sounds like something I don't need to know about," she said. "And look, a lot of lawyers would have folded with a judge putting that pressure on them. It's not right, but no one wants to make an enemy out of a judge. That'll put your career in the crapper faster than banging your client. Ledger, though, wasn't a brilliant lawyer or even a particularly good lawyer, but she was a stubborn bitch. So she just slogged on, and the jury liked her. They didn't like Grannick."

"What went wrong?" Ezra asked.

"Scandal," Vera said, spreading her hands palm up. "Like I said, Ledger was a workhorse. That meant a lot of mid-level slam-dunk cases, the bread and butter of the court system. Two-thirds of her cases, the opposing counsel cut a deal for their client because... they were fucking guilty, and it would be embarrassing to try and say otherwise. Only now, all of a sudden, a bunch of those clients had lawyered up with a real high-powered civil rights lawyer and alleged prosecutorial misconduct due to the use of jailhouse snitches."

"So she got pulled from the Grannick case," Ezra said.

"That she did," Vera said. "Her replacement offered Grannick a slap on the wrist deal right out the gate."

"Ledger got fired and blamed Charity for, what, dropping the lawyer the nod about her snitch problem?"

Vera shook her head. She hopped up off the desk and walked over to the briefcase she'd left propped up on the office's other chair. The brass latches clicked as she thumbed them open. She pulled out a sheaf of photocopied pages.

"Juicer than that," she said. "Ledger claimed she'd *never* used a jailhouse informant, but when the DA's office opened a review, they found dozens of them in her files. Most of them from a professional snitch who agreed to testify against her. At that point, I'd have accepted my guilt, and I know I didn't do it, but Ledger, the stubborn bitch, wouldn't back down. She accused the judge—Charity Parker—of setting her up and alleged Charity had some personal connection to Grannick. Which is when the shit really hit the fan for her because Charity took that very personally. Ledger wasn't just fired from the DA's office, she was effectively blackballed. Admittedly this is gossip, but a couple of the people I called backed it up. Between the scandal and Judge Parker's influence, she couldn't get hired anywhere. It wasn't worth the risk. This is a complete record of all the complaints that Ledger… ah… lodged at the clerk's office about Parker. She was convinced that an investigation would uncover significant judicial corruption. But she had no evidence, and we were in the middle of a pandemic, so they got filed and ignored. That did not stop Ledger. I should not have these, by the way."

She dropped the file on the table in front of Ezra. He picked it up and flicked through the pages briefly before he turned his attention back to Vera.

"So, Judge Parker wouldn't be pleased to see her at a big fundraiser?" he asked.

"From what I've heard, the only place Judge Parker would be happy to see Melanie Ledger is in hell," Vera said. "She was all set to move up in the judicial world two years ago, but all this made the powers that be hit pause. From what I've heard, she's set for a second bite at the cherry. The last thing she'd need is for anything to get in the way of that. Lucky enough, that won't be a problem anymore. Well, lucky for her. Not so much for Melanie, I guess."

She closed her briefcase and picked it up. It dangled from her hand as she looked between Clay and Ezra and raised a peppered gray eyebrow.

"I don't want to know why you asked, do I?"

"Probably not," Ezra said. "Bill us for your hours."

Vera gave him a *look*. "Well, I don't do this for love, dear. So obviously," she said, "my office will send it over. I really hope you didn't kill that poor girl. I think I would have liked her."

She turned and strode out of the office, her heels clicking against the floor.

"We didn't," Clay said. She looked back, and he shrugged. "Call it mommy issues. I don't want to disappoint unless I've earned it on my own merits."

She pointed a finger at him, the nail painted gray and pink. "You're a strange little man, Clay," she said.

"See?" Clay said as he swung his legs back up onto the desk. "That disappointment feels like it's worth something."

She shook her head and pulled the door open.

"One last thing," Ezra said. He held up the papers. "Did you come across the name Collymore in any of this?"

Vera tilted her head to the side and thought about it. "No," she said. "It doesn't ring any bells. Why?"

Ezra shook his head. "It doesn't matter," he said. "Thanks for this, Vera."

She waved her hand over her shoulder and left. The door swung shut behind her, and Clay waited for the click of heels to recede before he raised his eyebrows at Ezra.

"I gotta tell you, I figured Charity was fucking Collymore," he said. "All that overkill looked like a crime of passion."

"Or panic?" Ezra said. "Someone like Charity, they're either in control or out of control. No in-between. Look at me. There were a dozen different ways that Charity could have handled her laptop problem. Instead, she spiraled and put out a hit."

"Why now, though?" Clay asked. He leaned over the table and grabbed the stack of complaints to flick through them. "Two years and a couple of months, Ledger was yelling from the rooftops that Charity was crooked. No one listened. What changed?"

Ezra shrugged.

"Nothing?" he said. "That could have been the problem. Ledger was tired of not being heard, confronted Charity at her big party, and things got physical enough for her to end up dead."

Clay paused halfway through the complaints as something clicked with him. He flicked back and ran his finger down the page.

"Or," he said, "Ledger found some new information. Grannick was one of Fisher's men, right?"

Ezra sat forward, interested.

"Sort of," he said. "His father is one of Fisher's accountants. I'd guess it was a favor to get the kid off. Although I wouldn't have thought Grannick was important enough to merit the whole snitch conspiracy."

"What about Nesmith?" Clay asked.

He ripped one of the sheets loose, pushed it over the desk, and tapped his finger on the page.

Hal Nesmith, two years as an accessory after the fact.

"What do you want to bet that everyone on that snitch list was one of Fisher's men? It was a jailbreak. A legal one."

Ezra gestured for Clay to hand the list back. He glanced through it, his eyes flicking from side to side as he scanned for names. Then he shook his head.

"There's a couple, but Fisher's a big fish. Hard to be a professional criminal around here without doing a few jobs for him."

Clay folded his hands over his stomach. "It explains why she didn't call Fisher," he said. "If Ledger had the proof of something like that, she'd turn Charity from an asset into a liability."

Ezra picked the whiskey glass up and tossed it back.

"That happens," he said. "Kind of like your cleaner once Fisher got him in his sights."

Clay dropped his feet off the desk and stood up. "Don't tell me we broke up?" he said. "And I thought we were in it for the long haul."

The dregs of whisky sloshed against the side of the glass as Ezra toasted Clay. "Just getting your cock out of the clouds and back to reality," he said. "Don't convince yourself that he means more to you than he does. Because keeping Fisher on our side, that means a lot."

Clay braced his hands on the edge of the desk and leaned forward.

"And what if I decide Grade means more?" he asked.

Ezra looked pained and pinched the bridge of his nose between thumb and finger. "Warn me in advance," he said as he tilted his head back against his chair. "I can let the next person who comes for me just finish the job."

§

Clay ordered a coffee.

He figured it would counterbalance the beer he'd had before he left the Slap. The barista tried to upsell him on a Costa Rican blend with "notes of rosemary and wheat." He gave her a look over the counter.

"I asked for five shots of vanilla syrup and two hazelnut," Clay said. "Do you really think I'll be able to taste 'wheat'?"

The barista checked his order and nodded. "Fair point, I guess," she said. "I had to ask."

She made the coffee, handed it over, and Clay headed over to join Grade at the table by the window.

"Laptop?" he asked.

"I shipped it off to a hacker I know," Grade said. "They're going to rebuild some of it before they can access the hard drive. I wasn't expecting to need it again, so I didn't try to protect it."

"Anything will help," Clay said. "Once you get it up and running, it shouldn't be hard to find what we need. Based on Ledger's behavior, the files are only going to be a couple of weeks old."

"I'll let them know," Grade said.

Clay reached over the table and cupped Grade's face in his hand. He turned it to the side and scowled as he saw the fresh marks. There was a scratch high on his cheekbone, deep enough that it would linger for a while, and his split lip had fresh blood on it.

"What happened?" he asked.

Grade moved his chin out of the way. "I'm fine," he said. "Apparently, my face is extra slappable today."

Clay brushed his thumb over Grade's bottom lip and let the anger wash through him. He tried to gauge if he could really be professional and detached if Fisher did something to Grade.

Of course, the answer was yes. Clay knew how to switch on the emotional lidocaine drip that would make that work. It was the hangover that would fuck him up.

"What?" Grade asked as he reached up to cuff his fingers loosely around Clay's wrist. "What's wrong, Clay?"

It was *not* a good time to tell Grade the truth. Clay couldn't predict how he'd react. Maybe he'd take the calm, detached approach he took to dismembering corpses, or maybe he'd take a metaphorical ax to the wall of a motel bedroom. It was hard to tell.

"A lot of shit." Clay settled on that as an answer instead. He took Grade's hand and picked up his coffee to take a drink. "But I'm focused on the one that's going to hit us on the head first."

Grade was visibly dissatisfied with that, but a patrol car pulled up outside before he could ask any questions. Deputy Jones climbed out, adjusted his gun belt absently, and entered the coffee shop. He stopped just inside, the chimes over the door still murmuring, and looked around until he found Clay and Grade in the corner of the room.

He gave a quick, barely-there nod and went up to the counter to order. It was a plain cup of drip coffee from how quickly he got it, payment waved off by the barista, who probably hadn't tried to upsell him on the Costa Rican wheat. Jones carried it over with him to the seat at the table next to Clay and Grade, angled so he didn't look at them.

"Don't want to be seen with us?" Clay asked.

Jones got his notebook out and squinted at it. "No," he said into his coffee, "I fucking don't. Somebody with pull has it out for you, Traynor, Adams too. Your life is about to get very fucking uncomfortable. And don't ask me to cover your ass. This is above my pay grade."

"It's a generous pay grade," Clay said.

"Not generous enough," Jones said. "I got what you wanted this time, but that's it. Until this blows over, you don't know me."

Clay could have picked holes in that, but he refrained. It would be more satisfying to watch Jones flail when he realized a dirty cop didn't have the leverage to make that sort of call.

"And I was going to invite you to my birthday party," he said. "You talked to the cops in Doglan?"

Jones scratched the bridge of his nose with his thumb.

"You were right," he said. "Some weird shit went down with the Ledger case. The district attorney's investigators were all over it before the Dogleg cops had time to fuck it up themselves. They didn't even get to finish the inventory of the house before it pretty much got yanked out from under them. Apparently, they're concerned that Ledger had confidential information from her time in the DA's office. Disgruntled former employee and all that."

Grade looked nearly as uncomfortable as Jones. He still cleared his throat and asked, "So they wanted laptops, electronic devices, that sort of thing?"

Jones nodded. "Investigators seized all of that. It'll be handed back to the sheriff's department once they know there's nothing sensitive on there. Oh, except the laptop. There wasn't one.

Apparently the investigators would not let that go; it was a whole thing right there at the scene." He stopped and gave Grade a curious sidelong look. "Do I know you from somewhere?"

"No."

Clay stretched his legs out under the table and watched the traffic outside as it passed by the long window.

"What about the boxes in the garage?" he asked. "Did the investigators take them too?"

Jones shrugged. "Maybe," he said. "I didn't see anything about boxes, but like I said, the inventory wasn't even done before the scene got yanked out from under the locals. If it looked like paperwork, it was out of there."

"And Collymore?"

Jones paused as someone walked by the table on the way to the toilets. He took a drink of his coffee and tapped his pen against his notebook. Once the person was out of earshot, Jones licked his thumb and turned the page.

"Open and shut case," he said. "Just a guy with a nice car that thought he was Ryan Reynolds. He got carjacked and tried to fight back instead of giving that shit up to the insurance company. Stupid bastard. Had a wife and kid at home too."

"No record?" Clay asked.

Jones shook his head. "He had a juvie record, but it was low-level shit," he said. "Vandalism for tagging the school gym in Doglan after the team lost a match, driving without a license, and underage drinking."

Grade snorted. "I didn't even think they bothered to put that in your juvie file in Sweeny," he said. "Who wouldn't have one?"

That made Jones give him another interested look for a second; then he nodded his agreement.

"He's not wrong," he said. "But Collymore's dad had money. He wanted the kid to have a short, sharp shock, and everyone went along with it. Guess it worked, because the worst the guy got as an adult was the occasional speeding ticket. That it?"

"Files?"

"I'll leave 'em in the restroom," Jones said. "My payment?"

"I'll leave it on the table."

Jones drained his coffee, picked up his notebook, and headed toward the restroom. Clay waited until he was gone and then pulled an envelope out of his jacket. He set it down on the table next to his coffee.

"Looks like you were right," Grade said. "Whether Collymore was involved or not, Ledger's was the death that Charity cared about. And the reason is on that laptop. Charity must have figured that once Ledger was found dead, she could just have anything that looked like evidence seized under the fig leaf of confidential information. Only, none of the stuff she pulled out of the house scratched the itch, which left the one thing she didn't get, Ledger's laptop. What I don't get, though, is if Ledger had all this? Why not just hand it over?"

Clay shrugged. A man in a green sweater stopped on the other side of the street, opposite the cafe, and took a picture. From the angle, it would catch Clay's car in the image.

Maybe he was just a tourist, but it wasn't exactly a scenic street.

"Because sometimes you just want to piss in someone's Cheerios," Clay said. "Ledger got wind that Charity was going to make her big announcement about running for election to the Kentucky Supreme Court, and she didn't want her to enjoy it. So she turned up to tell Charity that she had finally found the proof.

Just so she could see the look on Charity's face in person when she heard the news."

Grade shook his head. "I never get that."

"Spite?"

"Of course not. You've met my sister," Grade said. "I mean the number of people who do something that will definitely make someone want to kill them but never seem to expect that it might get them killed."

"That's the human condition," Clay said. He took a drink of coffee and stood up, just in case Jones pissed like a firehose. "I'll be back in a minute."

Grade nodded. "I'll get on it."

Clay left him at the table and headed down to the restroom, crossing paths with Jones at the door. He picked the heavy manilla envelope up off the tank of the toilet and tucked it into his jacket.

Corruption was always much easier to stomach when it was on your side.

When he left the restroom, Jones was gone.

Clay headed back to the table and sat down, just as his phone went off in his pocket. He pulled it out to answer it, and Ezra growled in his ear.

"Heads up from the courthouse," he said. "Judge just signed off on a search warrant for our property. That's not going to be a problem, is it?"

"Hope not," Clay said. He hung up and lifted his coffee to finish the last syrupy dregs. "Talking about people who got themselves killed, though. Might be a good time to clean house at mine and Ezra's. Before we get any unannounced visitors."

Grade hesitated for a second.

"We'll pay the going rate," Clay said as he put the cup down.

"You should lead with that," Grade said. He left his cup half full of tea and got up. "Ezra's first, then we can go to yours."

"That's hurtful," Clay said as he put his hand on the small of Grade's back as they headed out. "Not going to lie."

"I like you more," Grade said, "but the transfers come from his bank account, so I don't want it frozen. For a start, you're about to buy me a new van."

CHAPTER THIRTEEN

SWEAT SOAKED GRADE'S T-shirt. The fabric was plastered to his back as he dragged the dead man in the duct-taped-up trash bags down the stairs, his plastic-covered heels thumping rhythmically on the wood.

He'd been right. Ezra's house had been easy. A broken neck was a gift when you were in a hurry. All they'd had to do was roll him up in a rug and chuck him in the back of the shitty camper they'd pulled off Benny Quinn's secondhand car lot. It made Grade's neck itch to have a whole dead body back there in case they were stopped, but some shortcuts needed to be taken when there was a time crunch.

It left you open to making mistakes, but not as big a mistake as having a body on the scene when the cops got there.

Then Grade had broken the back window with his elbow to spray glass over the kitchen floor. He didn't have time to waste tidying up the mess that Charity's thugs had made of Ezra's house, so he would use it to his advantage.

Break-ins happened. Ask Melanie Ledger.

The cleanup at Clay's was going to take a bit more work.

Grade miscounted on the last step and stumbled for a second. He caught himself, but he dropped the corpse. The man's head hit the ground with a sickening, meaty crack.

"Anything I can do to help?" Clay asked.

"Give me a minute," Grade said.

He wiped his hands on his thighs, got hold of the corpse again, and hauled it down the hall to the garage. It wasn't going to stay there for long, but it gave Grade a chance to grab the crowbar that was propped up against the wall in the corner. It was dusty and sticky with cobwebs under his fingers as he looked around for the hammer he eventually found on top of the freezer.

He carried them both inside and held them up.

"Any preference?" he asked.

Clay crossed his arms and leaned back against what was left of the couch. He cocked his head to the side.

"Leg-breaking, the crowbar is always a good choice. It gives you a nice swing, and it's pretty intimidating," he said. "If you're going for joints, though, the hammer makes precision easier—"

"We're pulling up the floor in the bedroom," Grade said. That made Clay wince. Grade ignored it. "Crowbar it is. Come on."

He shoved the tool at Clay and headed upstairs at a jog. After a second, Clay followed him.

"What happened to solutions of eighty-four percent hypochlorite and sixteen percent peroxide?"

"Hydroxide," Clay corrected him. "And there's no time for that. So if we can't clean the evidence, we just get rid of it."

"Then what?" Clay asked as they got to work. If they'd been trying to do a good job, it would have taken longer. Since they weren't, the stack of splintered, broken floorboards built up quickly. "Bloody floorboards in the garage isn't any less suspicious."

Grade snorted. "Like Judge Parker reminded me, you can't get away from your roots," he said. They had to stop to move the bed, sheets already stripped and bleached. "We're going to do what any self-respecting country boy does with household garbage. Burn it in a pile of old tires in the backyard."

It took an hour and three texts from Ezra to strip the bedroom as the deputies carried out the warrants across Sweeny. They were lucky that there weren't enough deputies, even with some drafted in from Dogleg, to hit every property simultaneously. Grade had his fingers crossed that Clay's would be the last property on the list, but they weren't that lucky.

The bonfire of wooden floorboards was stoked and burning when Harry texted Clay that the patrol cars had just turned onto the road.

"Shit," Grade muttered. He tossed the bottle of kerosene to Clay. "Corpse is still in the garage. Stay here."

He ran back into the house and through to the garage, nearly wiping out on the floor as a ripped-up rug skidded under his feet. It took—his brain clicked over remorselessly as he hefted the bundled-up corpse into a fireman's carry on his shoulders—three minutes to get from where Harry had set up. That could work.

The corpse hung awkwardly over Grade's shoulders as he staggered to the garage door and hit the opener with his elbow. The door took a moment to think about it and then started to rise smoothly.

Every cop show Grade had ever watched played out in his head as he stood there. In those, the cops were always on the other side, waiting smugly. Grade bounced his heel and tried to keep a grip on the slick plastic. In the end, the tick of lost time in his head was too much to ignore.

He dropped the corpse to the floor, pushed it out under the door, and then got down to roll out after it.

No deputies waiting for him.

Grade dragged the corpse over to the camper, yanked the back doors open, and hoisted the body up and over the faded nicotine-yellow carpet on the floor. He dropped the man's head down just as he heard Clay's voice, pitched to carry, as it filtered through the house.

"I was starting to think you'd forgotten about me," he said. "I've inventoried the whiskey and the pharmaceuticals, so don't try and help yourself."

Grade scrambled over the body, the plastic slippery and the flesh rigor stiff under his trainers, and fell out the back doors. He landed hard on his hands and knees, scrambled up, and slammed the doors shut. The keys caught in his pocket as he dragged them out—Grade heard the fabric rip when he yanked on it—but he locked the doors just as a tall deputy walked around the side of the house.

She dropped her hand to the butt of her gun when she saw him. The twitchiness in her posture made Grade raise his hands smooth and slow.

"Who the fuck are you?" she asked, then didn't wait for an answer. "Turn around and put your hands against the vehicle."

Grade did as he was told. A shove between his shoulders pinned him against the doors of the camper, his cheek pressed against the glass of the window. He stared through a crack in the curtains he'd not noticed before at the trash-bag-covered foot of the corpse as an impersonal hand frisked him

"Anything in your pockets?" the woman snapped. "Knife? Needles? Am I going to get a fucking STD if I put my hand in?"

"No, ma'am," Grade said.

The search didn't bother him in the same way that dead bodies didn't bother him. It should, but his brain didn't think he had time for that, so it just flicked that bit off. The counselor the school had made him go to said that was a maladaptive reaction, but he'd been paid barely above minimum wage to do shit-all about bullying, so what did he know. It seemed adaptive enough to Grade.

The contents of his pockets—a couple of dollar bills, the keys to his van, a condom—were thrown onto the ground. Once she was satisfied, she stepped back and told Grade to turn around. She had his wallet in her hand, flipped open, and his license between her fingers.

"Thomas Pulaski," she read out. "That you? What's that face for?"

Grade rubbed his hand over his mouth and chin. "I was named after my dad," he said. And no one had called him that since he was at school. It didn't even feel like his name anymore. Tommy Pulaski was a skeleton in a trashed muscle car somewhere, not him. "It's a sore subject."

She grunted and pulled him to the side so she could try the door of the camper. When it didn't open, she gave it a yank, one foot braced against the fender, but the lock held.

"Open it," she said.

Another deputy came around the side of the building, Clay in cuffs ambling along behind him.

"Fowler," he said. "What's this?"

"One of Traynor's employees," she said. "I caught him out here at this camper, sir."

"He doesn't do it for money," Clay interjected.

"Shut up," the senior deputy told him. He nodded to Grade. "Open it."

"Do you have a warrant?" Grade asked.

The deputy looked annoyed.

"We do," he said and pulled the warrant out of his jacket. He handed it to Grade. "Now, open the van."

Grade unfolded the warrant and looked it over. "This is for Mr. Traynor's property," he said, "not mine."

"Don't split hairs with us," Fowler snapped. She grabbed his shoulder and yanked him over to the van. "Open it."

"He has a point, Paul," Clay said.

The senior deputy—Paul—made an annoyed sound in the back of his throat. "Shut up, Clay," he said. Then to Fowler, "He's right. We don't want any fuckups on this once we get to court. Everything by the book, Fowler."

"What?" Fowler protested. "Sir, he was obviously out here to hide something."

"Get Reyes around here with his dog. If there's anything in there, that'll give us probable cause for a search," Paul told her. "I'm afraid your friend is not making things any better for you, Clay."

Clay grinned, loose and easy. "He doesn't usually try," he said, "so that's nothing new."

Paul looked annoyed and shook his head. "If there's anything to find, we'll find it," he said. "Maybe you won't find this situation so funny then."

Grade sat on the hood of one of the patrol cars, cuffed after all, and watched with interest as the deputies went through Clay's house with a fine-tooth comb. He'd not seen a search warrant enacted since his dad died, not in person. He did keep up on procedure. It was interesting to watch. He could see a few places that he could take advantage of in his, ah, usual capacity.

Every now and then, one of the deputies would swing by with a question.

Clay crouched on the ground, hands cuffed behind him, and fielded the questions as they came his way.

The drugs were his, and they were prescription.

The decision to redo the bedroom floor had been impulsive.

He did not own a camper van.

Finally, Paul came back over. He looked frustrated.

"What happened to the house?" he asked. "It looks like someone has turned it over already."

Clay shrugged. "I lost my shit," he said. "Trashed the place. I got PTSD and a drink problem, Paul. Shit like that happens."

"Sounds healthy," Paul said. He turned to go, but Clay whistled him back.

"You know this is bullshit, right?" he asked.

Paul hooked his thumb into his gun belt and looked down at Clay. "I know you're criminals."

Clay shrugged that off. "Prove it," he said. "But no judge should have OK'd a warrant like this for… what? A fishing trip?"

Paul licked his lips and looked away. "It's unusual," he admitted. "That's why we're doing it by the book. You want a chair?"

Clay shook his head. "I'm fine," he said. "How was Ezra when you did him?"

Paul turned on his heel and stalked away.

"What was that?" Grade asked.

"He's Ezra's ex," Clay said, "so that wouldn't have been awkward *at all*."

Grade raised his eyebrows as he absorbed that bit of information. Before he could say anything, Reyes—based on the dog—came back around. He stopped to talk briefly to Paul and a visibly pissed-off Fowler, and finally shook his head and shrugged.

"Huh," Clay said. "Did you pay off the dog?"

Grade scooted forward to the edge of the hood and leaned down. "It's a drug dog," he said. "Most of them aren't double trained as cadaver dogs, especially if that's not what their trainer wants from them. I was mostly worried that whoever owned the van before it got to the lot had stashed weed in it somewhere."

The search didn't last long after that. No one apologized for the inconvenience before they left, but they did unlock the cuffs, so Grade supposed he couldn't complain.

He waited until the final cop car had driven out of there and then turned to Clay.

"What now?"

"We wait for the laptop," he said. "And you keep your nose clean, because the sheriff's department is going to be up our ass until we deal with Charity."

§

The sticker was gone, but other than that, the laptop looked good as new.

It had arrived that morning, delivered by private courier, in a box. The passcode and their report had been taped to the front of it.

"What does he fucking mean? There's nothing on here?" Ezra asked. He picked up the laptop and waved it around in frustration. "There has to be fucking something. Otherwise, why is Charity willing to kill for it? Is she just so cheap she doesn't want to pay for a new one?"

Grade hung back and listened while Clay flicked through the breakdown of what Angel had found on the laptop.

"I don't fucking know," Clay said. "Photos, letters to the various governing bodies, and a screenplay about a brave lawyer who was railroaded by the system, but that's it."

Grade tucked his hands into his pockets.

"Maybe there was a clue in the screenplay?"

Clay shook his head. "It was apparently 'not bad,' and he could see Sandra Bullock in the lead role, but it wasn't finished. The story ends when the lawyer is fired. No hint as to how she got her own back."

Ezra stalked away from the table. "So it's fucking useless?" he said as he threw the laptop on the top of the bar. It skidded along the polished wood and knocked over a few shot glasses. Ezra ignored the clatter as he grabbed a beer from the shelf. He tossed it to Clay and then got another for himself. "The Slap has been closed down three times in the last week. It ain't even worth opening the Choke because no one wants to drive past three patrol cars before they can get their titty fix. And you know what?"

He popped the cap off the bottle against the bar and took a swig, then wiped his mouth on the back of his arm.

"That's fine. I know what I am and what I do. That's the cost of doing business in our line of work," he said. "But they stopped me on the fucking school run. I had to call Janet to come and get the kids. Ally's started wetting the bed again. Fucking bastards."

Grade bit his tongue on the urge to ask if it had been Paul who'd stopped them. Sometimes he didn't have to make things worse. It was a new thing he was trying.

Harry was propped up against the wall by the window to keep a lookout on the street. Ezra had not been joking about the number of times deputies just rolled by.

"Maybe the laptop is a red herring?" he suggested. "From what you say, Judge Parker has danced to Fisher's tune for a while. She might be sick of being in people's pockets."

Clay tossed the papers down on the table. He stretched and cracked his neck, then pulled out a packet of cigarettes. "She probably is. But she sent the DA's investigators to get the laptop. It was only when they didn't find it that she got angry."

Ezra eyeballed Grade for a moment, but didn't point out that technically made it Grade's fault. For once.

"What if it wasn't the judge who was sick of it?" Grade said. He paused as everyone looked at him, but he pushed on. "Two years. That's how long Ledger had been looking for something to use against Judge Parker, and what did she have?"

"Fuck all, apparently," Ezra said. "Which means we do too."

"Exactly," Grade said. "Clay thought that Ledger went to the party that night so she could throw what she knew in Charity's face. What if he's right, but she lied? Two years and she had nothing, so she just turned up and *told* Charity she had the evidence. That she knew. And Charity's guilty conscience did the rest."

Ezra nodded. "That makes sense," he said. "It doesn't *fucking* help, though, does it?"

Clay swung onto the back legs of the chair. "Maybe it does. Think like a law-abiding citizen, Ezra. Charity doesn't want to believe that she didn't need to beat a man to death with a fucking wine bottle, so as far as she's concerned, the laptop is still a ticking bomb. We know it's a shit screenplay and some photos of food, but she doesn't."

Ezra considered that for a second and then grimaced. "Except she's still a judge, and we ain't Fisher. We don't have the resources to move against her without ending up in federal prison. That's why we needed the evidence, so the fucking legal system could work for us for once."

There was something there. Grade took Clay's beer off him and took a drink. He licked his lips and hesitated for a moment, because this was not his wheelhouse. It went against everything he stood for professionally—which was being reliable, so people kept giving him money.

"What if we need to stop thinking like law-abiding citizens," he said slowly. "We helped Judge Charity Parker get away with a double murder. Why don't we just make that right?"

Ezra squinted dubiously. "You want us to confess?"

"No," Clay said. He brought the legs of his chair down onto the floor and turned to look at Grade. "I think he wants to frame Charity for a murder she *did* commit."

Grade nodded. "Pretty much," he said. "We just tighten up the story."

§

"What?" Cody said. He grabbed the tickets out of Grade's hand and then whooped. "You bought us tickets to Hurricane Bay? Uncle Grade, you rock."

Susie gave Grade a curious look. "Is it really a good time?" she asked.

At the same moment, Dory protested, "I can't afford that! I appreciate the thought, but there's travel and hotels and food and—"

"Mooom," Cody protested. "Come on."

Grade held up his hands. "It's the best time. The Choke's closed, so it's not like she'll lose any money. I paid for the hotel already, and I'll give you gas money. All you have to do is pay for food."

Cody bounced in his chair. "I can pay for that!" he said. "I've money saved from Christmas and birthdays and when Uncle Grade gives me money for lunch."

Dory hesitated. "I don't know," she said. "I can't accept this."

Grade shrugged. "You have to," he said. "I got the cheapest hotel I could find. No refunds. I think the three of you need to get away, have some fun."

"You're not coming?" Cody asked as he looked up at Grade. The disappointment in his face stung a bit. There weren't that many people in the world who wanted to spend time with Grade; he hated to let one of the few down. "But it'd be fun."

Grade ruffled his hair. "It'd be awesome," he said. "But I have work. Maybe next time."

Cody pouted, but the lure of the water park distracted him after a second. He scrambled to his feet. "I'm going to go pack!"

"I haven't said yes, yet!" Dory protested after him as he left the kitchen. She waited for the door to swing shut and then narrowed her eyes at Grade. "How much shit are you in?"

"Dory! Language," Susie protested on autopilot.

"Mom, stick it," Dory said. "This once, you don't get to pretend that this is fine. He's not the Artful Dodger. Neither was Dad. This is real, and people get hurt."

For a second, Susie looked injured. Then she lifted her chin. "You think I don't know that?" she asked. "You think that I don't know what probably happened to Tommy? That Grade doesn't deliver Uber for ten grand a night?"

Dory looked at her. "I know you know," she said. "You just *pretend* you don't and that it's all OK. Well, maybe it isn't. Is this to do with the sheriff's department being all over the Choke?"

Grade hesitated. "I can take care of myself," he said. "You're the ones I'm worried about."

"I'm not going anywhere," Dory said. She sat back and crossed her arms, her face set in a pout. "You think that we'll be safe if we go? That we won't get hurt as long as we're not here when something happens to you? You selfish little bastard."

Susie slapped her hand on the table. "Enough," she said. "We're going."

"You can't make me," Dory said.

"He's already paid," Susie said. She pushed herself up and brushed her blouse down over her stomach. "I'm not going to waste that money. Go and pack, Dory. Whatever it is you need to get off your chest, it can wait. Your brother needs some time."

She waited.

"Dore," Grade said. "Please."

"Assholes," Dory said as she got up stiffly. "You're all assholes. But fine. We'll run and hide, and if I have to bury you when we get back, Grade? I'm putting Tommy on the gravestone and telling everyone all your secrets."

She slammed out of the room.

Susie started to follow and then hesitated. She reached out and touched Grade's cheek, the bruises now faded to browns and blues. "If there's anything I can do to help," she said, "even if it's going away, I'll always do it for you."

She turned to go. Grade cleared his throat to stop her, then hesitated when she turned back around. The last thing he wanted was to get his family involved. But it would make things easier if…

"Mom," he said, "do you ever do any cleaning work up on Longwall?"

She cocked her head to the side in confusion but nodded without asking any questions.

"Greta has the contract for most of those houses," she said. "Why?"

"I need to get into one," he said. "I'd rather not break anything."

Susie went over to her red coat hung on the back of the kitchen door and fished out a set of keys.

"Greta keeps all the keys at the office," she said as she handed the set over. "We have to drop them back by eight and pick them up every morning at four. Greta can never be bothered to get up that early, so we all have our own keys to get in. Wear gloves. I don't want to lose this job."

She squeezed his hand and left.

Grade bounced the keys in his palm for a moment and then got up and left before Dory came back to yell at him again.

CHAPTER FOURTEEN

CLAY STOOD POOLSIDE at Fisher's estate and watched Nesmith cut through the water. After the third lap, Nesmith gave in and boosted himself out onto the side. He sat, dripping water onto the tiles, on the edge of the pool, and looked Clay up and down.

"Like what you see?" he asked as he wiped water off his chest with his hand.

Clay considered that for a second and then shook his head.

"There is no answer that won't blow up in my face, is there?" he asked.

Nesmith leaned back and braced his arms behind him. "Probably not," he said. "But if you turn up unannounced, you have to deal with awkward moments like this. Why are you here, Mr. Traynor?"

Clay grabbed one of the poolside loungers and dragged it over. The legs scraped noisily against the tiles. He dropped it next to the pool and sat down on the edge, his elbows braced on his knees.

"You know about the trouble we're having right now?" he said. "With the sheriff's department?"

Nesmith nodded. "You work for us now," he said. "We keep tabs. It sounds like they've pretty much shut you down."

"No one can take a piss without getting slapped with a public indecency," Clay said.

"Teach them to use the inside toilets," Nesmith said. "That's one problem solved. Anything else I can help you with?"

"Business is slow," Clay said. Then he shrugged and corrected himself. "Make that business has been stopped. We can carry our obligations for a while, but—"

Nesmith held up his hand to cut Clay off.

"You think that's our problem because you won't be able to pay us what you owe," he said. "Am I right?"

Clay scratched the back of his neck. "Before you get long-winded," he said and reached into his jacket, "my problem is this."

He handed Nesmith the warrant, pages already folded back so he could see Judge Charity Parker's signature on the dotted line.

"I think that's our problem," Clay said. He reached over to tap the signature. "Parker is bought and paid for, so why is she fucking with us?"

Nesmith stared at the paper for a moment. His fingers tightened enough that the damp paper creased and ripped under his grip. He grimaced and handed the warrant back to Clay as he got up.

"That is not something that we initiated." He picked up a robe from the back of the chair and pulled it on. In general, he wasn't Clay's type—he liked them tighter wound but less buttoned-down—but the way the silk stuck to wet skin was kinda hot. It was not the time to be distracted, though. "Parker *is* an officer of the court in her day job. Signing warrants falls under her authority."

Clay scratched his jaw with his thumb. "Good to know it's not Fisher using his influence to run us out of business," he said.

"You might want to spread the word on that because it'd be easy for someone to get the wrong end of the stick."

Nesmith tied the belt of the robe loosely around his waist. "Don't tell me," he said. "You're going to make sure they find that stick?"

Clay stood up and brushed his hands over the seat of his jeans.

"Not like I need to," he said. "Parker was the prime mover behind this 'starve 'em out' policing they're using on us. You own her. If she didn't do it with your backing, she did it to curry favor."

Nesmith's expression curdled. He picked up a towel and dried his hands and hair quickly. Then he held out his hand for the warrant.

"I'll look into it," he said. "If Parker overstepped, Fisher will deal with it."

"He better," Clay said. "First Buchanan, now your pet judge. It doesn't look good, does it."

Nesmith's jaw tightened.

That could have been a little far, Clay conceded to himself. It was too late for second thoughts. He handed the warrant over to Nesmith.

"Tell Fisher I hope he enjoyed his cake," Clay said. "See you around, Nesmith."

Clay turned and left. When he looked back, Nesmith had stalked up the garden and was headed into the house. It was hard to tell from a view of his back, but he walked like he was pissed.

Mission accomplished.

§

Clay lost his tail halfway back to Sweeny. The nondescript gray sedan got cut off by a truck, stuck in a slow convoy of traffic, and missed when Clay took the first exit off the road.

Amateurs.

He pulled onto the side of the road and dropped one foot to the ground to brace the motorbike. His gut ached, scar tissue spasmed into knotted, tender bands, and he tried to stretch it out as he waited.

A turkey waddled out of the tree line, gave Clay a disgruntled look, and fluffed itself out importantly. It gobbled at him as it fanned its tail and drooped its wings to trail in the dirt.

Clay watched it for a second and then pushed back his jacket to reveal the gun holstered under his arm.

"I can take you," he said.

The turkey paced around in a circle and took a short run at him, its chest puffed out and ruffled. When he didn't react to the aggression, the bird thought better of it, shook itself, and headed back into the trees.

"You're lucky I always hated Thanksgiving," Clay told it as he let his jacket fall back over the gun. The sound of a car engine drifted up the road and caught Clay's ear. "Finally."

He pushed the bike back upright and revved the engine. The back wheel fishtailed briefly in the dry dirt at the side of the road, kicking up a cloud before it finally grabbed some traction. Clay tightened his thighs around the bike as it surged forward, and he pulled back onto the road.

This time when he checked his rearview mirror, the car was back.

Clay kept an eye on the speedometer all the way back to Sweeny. He didn't want to lose them again.

Everything was going according to plan. Right up until the black Chevy going the other way down the road suddenly swerved over the white lines. It clipped the bike, Clay's leg pinned against the driver's side door, and for a *second*, Clay thought he could recover. He could feel where he needed to shift to rebalance the bike.

Then it all just spun out from under him. He hit the road hard, bike on top of him, and they scraped along the concrete in a shower of sparks and smoke. Something in Clay's knee went loose and hot as it pulled in the wrong direction, and he felt it give. It didn't hurt yet. That was a bad sign.

He slammed to a stop against the Welcome to Cargill County sign, hard enough he felt the metal struts buckle. That hurt. Then the bike slammed to a stop against him, his holster jammed so far into his side he figured he'd see the imprint for a year, and he felt the sharp, almost heady bloom of pain as his ribs compressed around his lungs.

Pain had an audio track. People never talked about it, but it crackled through his ears like static and drowned out the world around him. Clay grabbed the saddle of the bike and pushed at it. The weight of it didn't shift.

He dropped his head back to bounce against the road and screwed his eyes shut as he tried to focus.

The singsong inflections of someone in the middle of panicking cut through the static first.

"Jesus Christ. Jesus *Christ!*" someone repeated. It took Clay a second to place Errand Boy. "What did you do? You've killed him. We weren't supposed to kill him. Judge Parker was very clear and—"

"She was," someone else said calmly. "To us. He's more useful alive, but he's less trouble dead. Something he should remember."

Clay tried to shift the bike again. This time it moved enough he could squirm out from under it. He used the sign to pull himself to his feet, his chest tight and unhappy about him breathing.

"Remember? I should get that stitched and framed," Clay said. "That's the family motto."

He spat blood onto the fuel tank of his bike and took stock of Charity's new muscle. Five of them, if you counted Errand Boy. The other four were masked, black gaiters pulled up over their mouths and noses. They looked like cops to Clay. They just carried themselves like it; it was in the way they moved as they fanned out around him.

"Get down on your knees," one of them said as he pulled a gun from under his jacket. He pointed it at Clay and used the muzzle to point to where he wanted Clay to go. "Now!"

The Kentucky accent cracked into something thicker, the Pashtun edge harsh as a dead man echoed the words. His brain cast a shadow over the scene because it had been nighttime when it happened, and he could smell smoke and charred meat.

That had been him. Clay sliced bacon, scraped off to cook on the fire-melted sand.

Clay grinned, blood salty and slippery on his teeth, and drew his gun in one smooth, easy motion. The muzzle was rock steady as he pointed it back at the masked cop. He hurt—some places more than others—but he'd felt worse.

"What if I don't?" he asked.

The leader shook his head. Despite the mask, he managed to look contemptuous.

"You can't shoot us all."

Clay winked at him. "But I can shoot you."

And he did. He aimed low and to the side. The last thing he wanted was the complication of a dead cop if he didn't need it. The bullet punched through the leader's thigh and blew out the back. Blood sprayed out in a fine mist that splattered over Errand Boy's hands and white shirt

He squawked. The leader yelped and staggered back into the car, his weight on one leg as he grabbed at the hole in his thigh with his bare hand.

"Get him!"

Clay could have probably taken out Errand Boy, who looked increasingly terrified by how things had turned out, but he hesitated, and the other three swarmed him before he could pick a new target. One of them yanked the gun out of his hand and tossed it to the side. It bounced away into the undergrowth.

Two of them grabbed him by the arm and tried to wrestle him to the ground. The third threw a punch that caught Clay on the side of the face. It would have broken Clay's jaw if he'd not yanked his head back.

He threw his head to the side and smacked his skull into someone's face. A strangled yelp followed the distinctive crackly pop of a broken nose, and the grip on Clay's arm loosened. He yanked his arm free, twisted in one smooth motion and shoved his thumb into the second man's mouth, crooked into his jaw like a fishhook. Clay yanked to the side and banged the man's head off the damaged sign. The thin skin of the man's forehead split open on the metal, and blood dripped down his face. Now both hands were free.

Clay stepped forward quickly, and… Nope. His knee wasn't having that. He could have worked through the flare of eye-watering pain. Clay had felt worse. The fact it just folded—the wrong way—under him threw him more. Before he could recover, the third guy grabbed him by the shirt, fingers knotted in the cotton, and threw another punch.

This one connected squarely on Clay's temple and washed gray-tinged red over his vision. His head went blurry, and when it cleared, he had his fist clenched around the third man's balls, the zipper of his chinos rough against Clay's hand, and his thumb jammed into the man's eye socket.

Stupid really.

Clay had never been particularly squeamish. That was one of the things that had impressed his training officers in boot camp, that hurting people didn't make him flinch. Eyeballs always made him quietly gag, though. It was the way they gave under pressure, the wet give of them as they shifted in the eye socket. He tasted bile in the back of his throat as he pressed down.

The third man's mouth fell open on a howl as he writhed. Before Clay could dig in that last, necessary bit of pressure, something cracked on the back of his skull.

This time when his vision grayed out, it didn't come back. He dropped into the dirt, scratchy against his face, and briefly felt hands on him before his brain decided to reset and just switched off.

§

Everything hurt when Clay woke up.

He blinked groggily and licked dry lips as he took stock of himself. His knee throbbed, a hot, sickly pain as the leg of his jeans squeezed around it, and his head hurt. Both hands, currently cuffed behind his back, stung itchily. Road rash, probably.

Clay cracked his neck and then worked his jaw from one side to the other until the joint clicked and loosened. He rolled his shoulders back and straightened up on the chair he'd been dumped on. The man next to him pulled the needle out of Clay's arm, a quick scratch as a drop of blood ran down Clay's forearm and got lost in the ink, and scrambled backward.

He looked around at the bare metal walls and the few damp-stained boxes stacked against them.

"Shipping container," he said. "Good choice. Blood'll hose right off."

Charity Parker gestured for Errand Boy, blood still on his clothes, to pull a chair over. He did so uneasily, his attention on Clay, as if Clay might snap his cuffs and lunge at any moment.

"Stop it," Charity told him impatiently. "Even with the speed we just gave him, the man can hardly sit up straight, never mind do anything to you."

Errand Boy muttered an apology and stepped back. He wiped his hands nervously, scrubbing with his fingers at the already raw skin. Clay winked at him.

"I didn't want it to be this way," Charity said. She glanced at the smartwatch on her wrist, absently tapped the screen, and turned her attention back to Clay. "All you had to do was give me the laptop. But no. Not you. Did you think you could use it for leverage?"

Clay settled back in the chair. Speed always made him mellow, like someone had smoothed down the hackles on a dog. It evened all his moods down, leveled him out.

"You'd have tried to have us killed anyhow," Clay said. "You couldn't let Fisher know you'd left a paper trail that would implicate him in judicial corruption. That would get you taken with him on a trip to feed the fishes, wouldn't it?"

Charity's mouth twisted in an unpracticed grimace, her glossy lips pinched in against her teeth. It was an ugly expression. It looked more real than her usual practiced mask.

"I'm not one of you," she said. "I'm not *disposable*. You can't pick up another one of me in any shitty bar in this county. I used Fisher, not the other way around."

"Keep telling yourself that," Clay said.

Her hands clenched hard enough Clay would bet she cut her palms, but then she pointedly relaxed them and sat back.

"I had hoped that your cleaner would hand it over," she said. "Then we could have been done with this."

Clay ignored that. "I'll be honest," he said. "I assumed you were fucking Collymore, he broke it off, and you went *Fatal Attraction* on him. Ledger just walked in at the wrong time. I mean, put your all into killing Collymore, didn't you?"

Charity swallowed hard. Her expression was somewhere between horror and a queasy excitement. She flexed her hand for a second, as if she could still feel the neck of the bottle. Then she turned the gesture into smoothing down her skirt.

"None of that was meant to happen," she said. "None of it would have happened if Melanie Ledger had just taken the loss like a big girl. But she thought she could beat me, that she deserved something from me."

"She did beat you."

Charity gave him a bleak look. "What did you talk to Fisher about?"

"I read that biopic they did for you in *Kentucky Monthly*," he said. "Born rich, Daddy lost all your money—"

"Dad died," Charity corrected him. "He would have recouped his losses; he always did. Mom just didn't understand money the way he did."

"Bet that's what went through your mind when Melanie confronted you," Clay said.

"Did you tell Fisher about the laptop?" Charity yelled. Her voice bounced off the inside of the box, and Clay winced. He would have rubbed his ears if he had a hand free. "Does he know? Is that why he keeps calling me?"

"Maybe," Clay said.

The thing about losing your shit was that it took a *lot* to get there the first time. Once that trigger was pulled, though, it loosened up quickly.

Charity swung her head around and saw the steel rails stacked up next to the wall. She stalked over, grabbed one, and swung around with it cocked back at waist height like it was a badminton racquet.

"Does he know!" she demanded.

"Not yet," Clay said. "I was just there to set up the meeting for Ezra. It's not information he's going to give away for free. Been a bit rough, the last few weeks."

"If you'd handed the laptop over, it wouldn't have been necessary," Charity said. "You brought this on yourself."

"You tried to have us killed."

Charity dropped the rail. It hit the floor with a clatter.

"Where's the laptop?" she said.

"Why should I tell you? You're not going to let me walk out of here."

Charity brushed dirt off her palm. "No," she admitted. "But I can have you killed, or I can leave you here to rot. They used this one for human trafficking, you know. It was one of my cases. Some of them died from asphyxiation. Others dehydration. It wasn't nice. The *smell* alone must have been horrendous."

Clay shifted in the seat and absently wriggled his hands. The plastic restraints had been pulled too tight. He could feel the itch of trapped blood in his fingers. This hadn't exactly been part of the plan. He was going to have to improvise.

"Ezra has it," he said. "It's in one of his garages in town, in the trunk of his ex-wife's car."

Charity looked triumphant for a moment, and then suspicious. "That was easier than I expected. I thought I'd have to ask one of our friends to soften you up. Isn't that how your kind of people put it?"

"No, we just call it torture," Clay said.

That made her flinch. It was funny how much distance people could put between what they were about to do and what it meant as long as they got to pick the words.

"I can be bought a lot cheaper than Grade."

Charity looked suspicious. He'd have thought less of her if she hadn't been. "You'd betray your partner? And your lover. For money?"

"Money and my fingernails," Clay said. "Ezra got us into this. It wasn't my idea. Getting into bed with Fisher wasn't my idea either. I don't want to die with the consequences of his actions, and there's no honor among thieves, Judge Parker."

"Fifty grand," Charity said.

Clay mugged resentment, but he wasn't in a position to haggle, so he finally nodded reluctantly.

"Deal," he said. "Babbage Auto Shop, off Armitage."

Charity's shoulders relaxed, and she exhaled in relief. Then she looked over at Errand Boy.

"I'll call you when I've got it," she said. "Then have Harris shoot him."

Errand Boy blanched until he was nearly whiter than his nice expensive shirt. "W...w...what?" he stammered. "I don't...I don't want to tell anyone that."

Clay flailed about in the chair and tensed his arms as he tried to bust the cable ties.

"We had a deal!" he yelled. "I gave you what you wanted. You can't fucking kill me."

Charity smoothed her hair down. "I'd have thought that too a couple of weeks ago," she said. "But it turns out I can live with it. It's not like any of you were useful. A failure. A parasite. A criminal. I'm not going to lose any sleep."

She stalked away, her heels loud on the metal floor, even over Clay cursing her the whole way. The door slammed behind her, and Clay relaxed. He slouched down in the chair and stretched his legs out in front of him. In about an hour, his hands would feel like they were in a vise, but right now, he could nap.

Oh.

He looked over at Errand Boy and jerked his head toward the doors.

"You'll want to wait outside," he said. "These usually block cell signals."

Errand Boy looked equal parts baffled and afraid.

"Are you really Catholic?" he asked.

It was a bit of an odd digression, but Clay supposed it was a valid question.

"Yeah," he said. "Not a good one, but that's not required."

Errand Boy nodded. "I'll pray for you."

He looked like he meant it.

"Go fuck yourself," Clay told him. "I can get to hell on my own."

DIRTY JOB

CHAPTER FIFTEEN

GRADE HAD GONE to school with Lennie "back then it was Gardener" Bennett.

He didn't remember her. That wasn't unusual. Grade had been a memorable kid—between the missing and/or dead dad and the pregnant sister—but he'd not had a lot of friends.

Apparently he'd gone to school with Harry too. Or at least been there at the same time.

"You have *no idea* how glad I am that you applied," Lennie said. She hooked her arm through Grade's as they walked down the corridor. Grade wasn't too sure how to go along with that— he didn't think anyone had ever done that to him before—but Lennie seemed happy enough. "You advertise for a morgue attendant, and I swear, the weirdos and the creeps just appear out of nowhere. Just disturbing people, Grade."

"I'm sure," he said.

Lennie shook her head, her glossy mane of honey-blond hair sliding over her shoulders. "And honestly, I think most of them would be disappointed. I know it seems like a creepy job, but it's not. It's just like any other workplace. We have paperwork that is never done, there's a lady in accounts who complains about the creamer every single week, and there's not that much difference between a dead body and a cardboard box."

Grade did think he might have liked Lennie if he'd gotten to know her when they were kids.

"I never thought of it that way," he said.

"I mean, if you *think* about it being a person once, that's different," Lennie said. "But if you don't, it's just another awkward thing to move from one room to the next. It's not like you touch them or anything."

She unhooked her arm from his and turned to point a finger at him while she took steps backward.

"Don't touch them," she said. "Do not touch the corpses. People will get really angry."

"Cross my heart," Grade said as he mimed the motion.

The smile was back as Lennie turned to push a door open; she had to put her shoulder to it to get it to move.

"Anyway, here we are," she said as she waved him into her office. "Head of HR, me. Who'd have thought it? I mean, it's just me and an intern from the high school, but still. Sit down. I'll get you the paperwork you need to—"

"Before we start," Grade said, "could I just use the restroom?"

Lennie rolled her eyes at him. "You did always have a tiny bladder," she said. "Always asked to go in the middle of class."

Maybe he wouldn't have liked her after all, Grade mused. He tuned out the directions to the restrooms—he'd memorized the layout weeks ago, for entirely different reasons—and finally managed to excuse himself out the door.

Instead of turning to the right, he went left. He walked back down the corridor until he got to the red box of the fire alarm. Grade smashed the glass with his elbow, pulled the lever, and then stepped into the storage room right next to it. He kept his sneakered toe shoved in the door to keep it open a crack as he watched for Lennie to go by.

It didn't take long. She hadn't wasted any time making sure that Grade was going to make his way out too.

Not that he wanted her to.

Once the halls were empty, Grade stepped out of the storage room and broke into a jog as he headed down the corridor. The ID he'd lifted from Lennie's jacket as she'd walked arm in arm with him got him through the door into the morgue. There were more drawers than Grade had imagined. He snapped on gloves and started to drag them open to check the toe tags.

Ferris, B.

Wallace, S.

Vernon, R.

Finally he found Collymore, F. They hadn't done an autopsy on him yet. It usually took a while for that request to go through. Grade pulled the drawer all the way out. The damage looked worse now, raised and livid against pale skin.

Grade dropped his backpack next to him and got to work. He plucked a couple of hairs out of the man's head and dropped them into a baggie. Then he pulled a syringe out of the pack.

There were a variety of injection sites on a body that were hard to find in an autopsy, but that involved injection before death. Dead skin was unforgiving. Plus, blood settled, which made it awkward.

Grade lifted the man's leg. It was stiff from the freezer, almost wooden. He slid the needle into the heel of his foot. No calluses to help disguise the puncture mark, but hopefully it wouldn't be remarked on. He drew out a syringe of cold, goopy blood and then bagged it too.

He was tempted to add evidence on the body, but that felt like hubris. There were smarter people than Grade in the world, although he didn't like to admit it.

Once he had what he needed, Grade bagged everything up and hitched his pack onto his shoulder. Then he hesitated as he glanced at Vernon, R.'s drawer.

Verne.

It couldn't hurt to check. Grade pulled the drawer open and took a quick look at Vernon. He was a big, heavyset man with dirty-blond hair and a ginger beard. A brief scan of his body made it look like he'd died after an impact with a car. The bruise patterns across the backs of his thighs and the bloody injury on the back of his head matched.

Just another accident.

Probably.

The only thing was that Grade had seen Vernon before. At the Slap, talking to Ezra.

Grade hesitated for a second as he wrestled with that, but a mental "nudge" served as a reminder that he didn't have much time left.

He laid Verne back down, closed the drawer, and left.

There were cameras at the two main exits, but not the fire door at the back of the building. Grade took the steps down three at a time and nearly wiped out in a puddle of spilled coffee on the landing. He caught himself and jogged down the last few steps.

The door had been left propped open with a fire extinguisher. Grade waited a second and then slid out and blended with the crowd.

He worked his way back around to where Lennie was, at the front of the building. She was on her tiptoes scanning the area and looked relieved when she saw him.

"What happened to you!" she said. "I thought you got stuck in the toilet. Again."

She slapped his arm and laughed. Grade shook his head.

"I had to… finish…" he said, clearing his throat as if it made him uncomfortable. "Then I got turned around, and then some guys dragged me along with them, and we came out the back. I wonder what happened."

"False alarm, apparently," Lennie said. She narrowed her eyes. "I bet it was Albert. He had his performance review today, and he's been desperate to skip it, but I've told him repeatedly, co-workers are like corpses, don't touch them."

Grade laughed genuinely and waited for the building to be cleared for them to go back in.

§

"I got a job," he said as he walked into the Slap. "But no one kidnapped me."

Ezra had finally gotten to the ER. He'd not needed surgery on his hand, but it was done up in a cast that his kids had covered with pink Sharpie kisses and dinosaurs. That Ezra didn't seem to give a crap what anyone thought about that was the most likeable thing about him as far as Grade could tell.

"No," Ezra said. He grabbed a leg of chicken from the bucket on the table. "They grabbed Clay instead."

"What?" Grade blurted. The kick of concern startled him a bit. It wasn't professional at all. "Is he OK?"

Ezra took a bite of chicken and wiped his mouth on a napkin. "They ran him off the road, so probably not," he said. "But Harry has eyes on the place they took him, so we just have to hope that the rest of the plan will still work. You sure you can get into Charity's house?"

Grade hesitated. It felt wrong. The thought of Clay being injured made him feel sick to his stomach, and more than just the usual queasiness from watching someone get hurt.

"If you want to help him," Ezra said, "make the plan work."

Grade took a deep breath, fished the keys out of his pocket, and dangled them from his finger.

"And as long as we get them back to the office by four, there's no reason for anyone to know we have them," he said. "Let's go."

§

They'd been at the judge's house for an hour when the sound of a car outside drew Grade to the window. He twitched the curtains back and peered out over the dark gardens. The gates at the end of the drive opened, and a silver BMW drove through them.

"She's here," he said.

Ezra tossed him the keys.

"I'll keep her busy," he said. "You go down and keep the gates open."

Grade took the servants' entrance out again and lingered in the doorway while he waited for Charity to haul her laptop and bag into the house. Once the door closed behind her, he headed down the drive to the gates. They didn't have to worry about the cameras. Grade supposed that Charity had a lot of guests she didn't care to have on video.

The cleaners had their own fob. Grade pressed it as he got close, and the gates swung slowly open again. He waited.

And waited.

He'd just started to fidget, his foot jittering as he imagined that everything had gone wrong, when the gold Lexus drove around the corner. Grade sighed in relief and stepped back to let it drive through the gates. Then he followed them up the drive to the big double garage.

The Lexus pulled up into the corner, and the engine died. After a second, the driver's side opened and Harry got out in a set of PPE.

Grade's stomach sank.

Then Clay scrambled awkwardly out of the passenger side in a similar outfit. Grade exhaled in shaky relief. His chest hurt. He started toward Clay and then hesitated. Give him a dead body to desecrate and he was confident, but social interactions were different.

"Fuck it," he muttered to himself. He ran over to Clay and pulled him into a quick, fierce kiss. Paper rustled as he pressed his body against it. Then he leaned back, one hand cupped around Clay's face, and tried to shove his brain back into work mode. "Did everything go according to plan?"

Clay grinned and dragged him back into a kiss, longer and more appreciative this time, until Harry pointedly cleared his throat.

"Everything except my knee," he said. "I think I tore something. Let's get out of here."

He slung an arm over Grade's shoulder and used him for support as they limped out of the garage and over to the nice black SUV that Ezra had stolen earlier that day. Grade got Clay into the back and let Harry take the front seat while he crawled in next to Clay.

After a couple of minutes, Ezra came out of the house. He had a black sleeve over his broken hand.

He swung up into the passenger side of the car and slapped the dash. "Let's go," he said.

"Did she see you?" Grade asked.

Ezra pulled the chloroform rag out of his sleeve and threw it into the glove compartment.

"No," he said. "Not that it matters."

Grade waited until they were on the road, nearly to where they turned off, before he called the police on a burner phone.

"Hi. Hey," he said. "This is probably nothing, but I was just jogging up Longwall and heard something going on in one of the houses. A lot of yelling… and I heard someone scream. Yeah, 298? They had a big party the other week. Look, I don't want any trouble. Just—no, I don't want to give my name. Just check it out."

He hung up and handed the phone forward to Ezra, who popped off the back and took the SIM card out.

"And now we wait," he said.

§

Grade perched on the end of Clay's new bed and flicked on the news. He sat through a story about an E. coli outbreak in schools and something about a marathon the mayor had run.

"Fucking Sweeny," he grumbled as he sprawled back on the bed. "Can't even get their scandals to run on time."

Clay limped in from the bathroom. He was supposed to use crutches until his knee was better, but he mostly left them propped in the corner of the room. His knee had managed to dislocate and then snap back into place during the accident on his bike. Lots of pain and swelling, some partially torn tendons, but nothing that wouldn't mend on its own.

He'd been more upset about the bike than his knee. It would be cheaper to get a new one, but he'd had the crushed wreck taken to a garage to be Frankensteined back together.

"It's not even been a week," he said. "Let it ride."

Grade sighed. "This is way more nerve-wracking than my usual gig," he said. "If that goes wrong, it's on the news the same day. 'Plastic drum of body parts dug up in desert by small child's dog.'"

Clay lowered himself onto the bed, jaw clenched as he stretched his leg out. The black brace strapped around his knee nearly hid the black-and-purple bruises. He held out his hand, and when Grade took it, pulled him up the bed.

"She's a judge," Clay said. He ran his hand up Grade's side, under his T-shirt. "They aren't going to rush to say anything. You need to try and think of something else."

Grade grinned as he sprawled on top of Clay's body, careful not to jostle his knee. He tangled his fingers through damp dark-blond curls and leaned down for a kiss.

"You think I need a hobby?" He ran his hands down Clay's arms, tracing the chaotic flow of the tattoos, and then pushed himself up so he straddled Clay's hips. He squirmed and felt Clay's cock thicken eagerly under him. Grade braced his hands on Clay's stomach, fingers spread on smooth tanned skin and the rougher slabs of scar tissue. "Any suggestions?"

Clay reached up to grip Grade's chin between his fingers and thumb.

"A few," he said as he pulled him back down into a kiss.

It was slow and easy. Or at least it started that way. Grade straddled Clay and rode his cock, his thighs and stomach tight as the muscles did the work. Deep, steady thrusts that spread his ass wide and licked heat along his nerve endings. Clay just sprawled back, hands behind his head and lip caught between his teeth, and watched through hooded eyes.

Until he lost patience with that. Then they ended up tangled in the sheets, Clay's hand around Grade's cock and his breath on his neck as he fucked him roughly. Grade made choked, wordless sounds as he grabbed the headboard with one hand to brace himself.

He came first, his come smeared up his stomach on Clay's fingers. Rather than finish, Clay pulled out of him and rolled over onto his back. He pulled the condom off and tossed it aside while he wrapped tattooed fingers around his cock to jerk himself off.

Grade lay next to him, sweaty sheets around his ankles, and watched with appreciation as he lazily caressed the rest of Clay's body, the taut, tensed muscles in his thighs and the flat, tawny buds of his nipples. He grazed a finger along the edges of the scars and followed them down to where they curled around Clay's hip.

"See?" Clay said, the words ragged as he came. He wiped his hand on his hip and then nodded at the TV. "A watched pot never boils."

The anchor on the screen put on his best serious face as he looked at the camera.

"Disturbing information continues to come to light after Sweeny's Sheriff's Department made a wellness check on Judge Charity Parker last week," he said. "Despite first impressions being the judge had been assaulted in her own home, it now appears that Judge Parker was somehow involved in the deaths of two people, one of whom was philanthropist and businessman, Franklin Collymore. Sources in the sheriff's department say that evidence found in Judge Parker's wine cellar suggests that he died there, and then his body was moved in a crude attempt to allay suspicion."

Grade sat. "Crude?"

"It wasn't your best work," Clay said. "You said that yourself."

"Still," Grade grumbled. "Do you think that's it? She could implicate us."

"If she starts talking to the police," Clay said, "Fisher will have her killed. He has enough pull to do it, and he can't afford not to once she starts making deals. Charity'd get a lot more from the district attorney selling him out than anything they'd offer for us. Plus, she can't prove a fucking thing."

Grade supposed that was true. He glanced at Clay and raised his eyebrows. Usually, Clay wasn't interested in anything but some distance after he'd come. He needed it to cool down. Not tonight.

"What?" Grade asked.

Clay reached for his cigarettes and lit one. He leaned back against the headboard and savored the first lungful of smoke. It eddied around his mouth as he exhaled.

"Fisher is going to be a problem."

"Because he lost his judge?"

"No," Clay said. "Because of you. He wants to know where your dad is."

"Tell him to join the queue," Grade said. "It starts behind me."

Clay shook his head and took a draw on the cigarette before he stubbed it out on top of the half-empty box. "That's not going to satisfy him," he said. "He thinks your dad is alive because, six months after he disappeared, your dad killed Fisher's brother."

Grade pulled away to the edge of the bed.

"That's bullshit," he said.

"Fisher doesn't think so," Clay said. "And that's what matters to Fisher. Is there any reason your dad would have killed Fisher's brother?"

Grade pushed his hand through his hair and cleared his throat. "Yeah," he said. "He had reason, but he didn't do it."

Clay looked at him. "I thought you'd not seen him since you left?"

"I haven't," Grade said. "But he couldn't have killed Fisher's brother."

"How can you know?"

Grade should have hesitated. It should have been hard to say; it hadn't been said in over a decade. Instead, it just slipped out as if it was easy.

"Because I did," he said. "I killed him."

Grade stared at Clay for a second as his brain tried to catch up with what his mouth—and parts further south apparently—had just done.

Dory was going to kill him, Grade thought bleakly, but at least it hadn't been the whole truth.

"What the fuck?" Clay asked.

ABOUT TA MOORE

TA MOORE is a Northern Irish writer of romantic suspense, urban fantasy, and contemporary romance novels. A childhood in a rural, seaside town fostered in her a suspicious nature, a love of mystery, and a streak of black humor a mile wide. Coffee, Doc Marten boots, and good friends are the essential things in life. Spiders, mayo, and heels are to be avoided.

TA Moore can be found at the following locations:
Blog: www.tamoorewrites.com

If you've enjoyed this book, please consider leaving a review for TA Moore on Amazon and other book retailer sites. Actually, it would be great to leave them for any book you've enjoyed. Authors truly appreciate it.

To catch up on all Rogue Firebird Press authors, please visit www.roguefirebird.com
For other TA Moore's Dreamspinner releases, visit www.dreamspinnerpress.com

Readers Love TA Moore

Bone to Pick (Digging Up Bones #1)

"If you like mystery, crime, super steamy sex scenes between two antagonistic men, and lots of intrigue, Bone to Pick definitely must be your next read."

—Love Bytes

Dog Days (Wolf Winter #1)

"… Flawlessly written… Each page was a new surprise, and this story was unlike anything I have read—I had no idea what would come next. Quite simply, I want more."

—The Novel Approach

Stone The Crows (Wolf Winter #2)

"… the second novel in the Wolf Winter series by T.A. Moore, and it's a stunner at every level and element. Horror, urban fantasy, and romance. There is nothing this author and book doesn't excel at."

—Scattered Thoughts and Rogue Words

Wolf at the Door (Wolf Winter #3)

"Cold and dark. Ferocious and unforgiving. Brutal and beautiful. This last instalment in the Wolf Winter trilogy takes all the pieces from the previous books and twists them some more into a finale that will take your breath away."

—Paranormal Romance Guild

AUTHOR CATALOG

**Published by Rogue Firebird Press
and Other Publications**

NIGHT SHIFT

Shift Work

Split Shift

Shiftless

ORANGE NORTHERN WOMAN SHORT STORY PRIZE WINNER

Island Life

(Ulster Tatler)

ORANGE NORTHERN WOMAN SHORT STORY PRIZE FINALIST

Words of Wisdom

*(Barefoot Nuns of Barcelona
& other short stories)*

ADDITIONAL PUBLICATIONS

Labyrinth of Stone

Red Milk

(Requiem for the Departed)

The White Heifer of Fearchair

(The Phantom Queen Awakes)

A Different Kind of Monster

(Blood Fruit)

HEX WORK
BY TA MOORE

My name is Jonah Carrow, and it's been 300 days since I laid a hex.

OK, Jonah Carrow isn't actually an alcoholic. But there's no support group of lapsed hex-slingers in Jerusalem, so he's got to make do. He goes for the bad coffee and the reminder that he just has to take normal one day at a time.

Unfortunately, his past isn't willing to go down without a fight. A chance encounter with a desperate Deborah Slater, and a warning that 'they're watching', pulls Jonah back into the world he'd tried to leave behind. Now he has to navigate ghosts, curses, and the hottest bad idea warlock he's ever met…all without a single hex to his name.

But nobody ever said normal was easy. Not to Jonah anyhow.

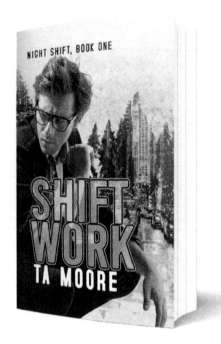

SHIFT WORK
BY TA MOORE

You'd think the werewolves would be the worst thing about the Night Shift; you'd be wrong.

All Officer Kit Marlow wanted was a cup of coffee and some downtime before his next night shift. Instead, he got a naked man in the elevator and an unaccounted-for dead girl in the morgue. He's going to need to deal with both before he can head for his bed.

Or anyone else's. Although not much chance of that.

Reluctantly partnered with the acerbic security consultant Cade Deacon—last seen naked in the elevator—Marlow delves into the dead girl's life. Between them, they uncover a new crime scene with the whiff of old corruption. A corruption that, five years ago, nearly took Marlow's life and ended his career.

Finding out who killed the dead girl on the slab might only be the start of this investigation. Oh, and it's the second night of the full moon. So 80% of the city, including Cade, will turn into werewolves in the middle of the case.

So, there's that.

WANTED – BAD BOYFRIEND
BY TA MOORE

His mother. His best friend. The barmaid at the local pub. Everyone is determined to find Nathan Moffatt a boyfriend. It's the last thing Nathan wants. After spending every day making sure his clients experience nothing but romantic magic, the Granshire Hotel's wedding organizer just wants to go home, binge-watch crime dramas, and eat pizza in his underwear.

Unfortunately, no one believes him, and he's stuck with lectures about dying alone. Then inspiration strikes. He needs the people in his life to want him to stay single as much as he does. He needs a bad boyfriend.

There's only one man for the job.

Flynn Delaney is used to people on the island of Ceremony thinking the worst of him. But he isn't sure he wants the dubious honor of worst boyfriend on the entire island. On the other hand, if he plays along, he gets to hang out with the gorgeous Nathan and piss off the owners of the Granshire Hotel. It's a win-win. There's only one problem—Flynn's actually quite a good boyfriend, and now Nathan's wondering if getting off the sofa occasionally is really the worst thing in the world.

BONE TO PICK
BY TA MOORE

Cloister Witte is a man with a dark past and a cute dog. He's happy to talk about the dog all day, but after growing up in the shadow of a missing brother, a deadbeat dad, and a criminal stepfather, he'd rather leave the past back in Montana. These days he's a K-9 officer in the San Diego County Sheriff's Department and pays a tithe to his ghosts by doing what no one was able to do for his brother—find the missing and bring them home.

He's good at solving difficult mysteries. The dog is even better. This time the missing person is a ten-year-old boy who walked into the woods in the middle of the night and didn't come back. With the antagonistic help of distractingly handsome FBI agent Javi Merlo, it quickly becomes clear that Drew Hartley didn't run away. He was taken, and the evidence implies he's not the kidnapper's first victim. As the search intensifies, old grudges and tragedies are pulled into the light of day. But with each clue they uncover, it looks less and less likely that Drew will be found alive.

Printed in Great Britain
by Amazon

84045439R00132